SOUL WEAVERS

A Compilation of Short Stories

SOUL WEAVERS

A Compilation of Short Stories

Anthony Trueman-Jones

Published by Custom Authors

Copyright 2013 © Anthony Trueman-Jones

ISBN 978-0-9574735-0-8

DEDICATION

This collection of short stories has taken me quite some time to complete and can only be accredited to a number of close friends who either inspired or encouraged me to finish the final product. These people are all very important to me, even if some are no longer in my life, therefore in case this ends up being my only book, I would like to dedicate this collection to the following friends:

Jane Ardielli
Laura Calvi
Marzia and Francesca Cavagnero
Lynn Harper
Manda "Bash" Mosley
Gary "Skin-Man" Skinner
Dale "Badger" Whitlock
Sarah Wiggle

And of course I dedicate this book to my beleaguered family who has had to put up with all of my questions and requests for constant feedback and reviews. They are my mother, Jenny McIntyre, my sister, Mandi

Camunak, and my fiancée, Stephanie "Stevie" Murphy. I would also like to include those who are sadly no longer with us and who are sorely missed, my father, Martin Jones, my uncle, Paul Williams, and my two grandmothers, Audrey "Nana" Williams and Mary Jane "Nan Jones" Jones.

Please let me know if you enjoy these stories through Facebook (Anthony Trueman-Jones) or Twitter (@TTruemanJones).

Anthony Trueman-Jones

CONTENTS

SHELTER ME

Shelter Me

Today is Sunday, the twenty third of July in the year of our Lord 1585, and in about ten hours time I shall be hung from the neck for a crime I did not commit.

Crouched in a small damp corner of my cell, I clutch to my naked chest a small wooden crucifix, its handle worn smooth from years of rubbing by thumbs of both the guilty and innocent. A creeping coldness threatens to numb my hands and feet as I start praying for salvation. Looking up to the small hole in the wall that serves as a pathetic excuse for a window, I watch daylight slowly transcend into twilight. This day that the Lord gave us has begun to end. I search the burning sky for a momentary glimpse of the sunset, possibly the last I shall ever see in this world.

Oh, dear Father, forgive me for my sins for I know not what I have done. I am but a simple blacksmith who has never asked anything from anyone and has always done my best at being fair and honest to even the smallest of your creatures, yet I am being punished. Why?

Oh, how well I remember that accursed night!

* * *

The air was chilled from the cloudless sky. As I looked up I felt countless stars send down their blessings. Work had been particularly demanding that day, and the only thing I'd longed for was the taste of Mr. Barli's finest ale down at the Queen's Head. As soon as my coals had cooled enough to be left, I donned my cloak and went in search of my simple pleasure.

A sudden scream quickly grabbed my attention. Looking around, I couldn't see anything unusual and so shrugged my shoulders, believing it to be nothing more than a cat. I continued on towards the Queen's Head. Suddenly the scream sounded again. This time it was longer, and I managed to locate it as coming from a side passage between two shops. Without thinking, I quickly ran to the sound.

At first darkness blinded me, so I waited, allowing my eyes to adjust. Two distant forms slowly appeared in front of me. By their movements, I could tell there seemed to be some kind of struggle. Carefully, I made my way forward, my eyes straining as they searched the shadowed ground for hidden obstacles. The cries grew weaker now, and I found myself concerned with the welfare of whoever was being attacked.

Something fragile suddenly snapped as I eased my foot down onto a wet piece of material, causing the attacker to spin round and face me. My heart froze as I looked into the bloodshot eyes of a city guard. In one hand he held the throat of a hunched form and in the other, a small knife.

"Leave me!" he uttered in a harsh whisper.

The hunched form stirred slightly, attempting to loosen the guard's grip. "No," it gasped.

"Quiet, bitch!" sneered the guard, then, staring into my eyes as if to enforce his will, he slowly repeated his order. "Leave … or die!"

Fear held my legs. I realised, even if I'd wanted to, I couldn't move.

"Help me, please," beseeched the captive. It suddenly dawned on me that it was female. Her hood fell away. Long dark hair spilled out across her shoulders and down her back. Looking down, I was immediately captivated by her beauty. Sky blue eyes, widened by fear, looked up to me. I saw her finely etched face stained with tears.

"I said shut it!" shouted the guard. Lifting the girl's head high and exposing her bruised throat, he lashed out, hitting her cheek with the pommel of his dagger. Blood splashed out across his gloved hand and down the side of his leering face. Mercilessly he threw her limp body into a stack of rotten crates.

Anger suddenly replaced fear. Screaming out my rage, I charged at the guard. Catching him completely by surprise, we both fell into a pile of refuse, but I was up against a seasoned fighter, not the local bully. Before I could even pull myself off him, a sudden explosion of pain hit my cheek, sending me sprawling backwards into the mud and filth. In next to no time, the guard was up on his feet and standing over me.

A well-aimed kick to my midsection brought another explosion of pain. This time I felt something give as I suddenly coughed up a warm liquid that left a strange taste in my mouth.

"Get up, boy!" he demanded. But all wind had escaped me, and I was finding it hard to draw breath.

Two rough hands grabbed hold of my tunic. I felt myself being lifted up to face the guard.

"Time to teach you how to take orders, boy," he sneered. I suddenly found myself facing the cold hard edge of his blade.

Panic released me from my groggy state of mind, and I quickly lashed out at him hoping to knock away his dagger. But I was clumsy and predictable as he blocked my reckless punch.

A lightning movement with his elbow and I was blinded by a sudden shower of brilliant stars. My nose crunched with a sickening sound as bone splintered. Thrusting out an unsteady leg, I desperately tried to regain balance as I felt the world start to spin. Alas my foot landed on a sodden patch of wet rags. I realised I was about to fall. Flapping my arms about wildly like some crazed chicken, I felt something sharp cut into my right forearm.

Unfortunately, my feeble efforts to gain balance failed. Landing heavily, I felt the wind inside me blast out with such force, that waves of nausea threatened to engulf me, and I soon found myself fighting the urge to be physically sick. It took several minutes but I finally managed to regain my composure. Wiping away the blood from my eyes, it dawned on me I should be dead. The guard was a trained fighter albeit a dishonorable one. The last thing I would expect from a person like him would be the chivalrous act of allowing his opponent a chance to regain both his strength and weapon. Carefully I looked around but I couldn't see him anywhere. Had he run away? No. I was a witness to an attempted rape or murder. He could not afford the risk of leaving me alive.

A stifled groan to my left caused me to search the shadows with bated breath. At first, I couldn't distinguish anything through the darkness, but then I noticed a crumpled form twitching to my right. Gingerly, for my rib cage felt as if it was on fire, I picked myself up and staggered towards the shape.

To my astonishment I found it was the guard. But why was he just lying there? Carefully, I turned him over. Horror quickly replaced my astonishment. I took an unsteady step back from him. Placed squarely in his stomach stood the cross piece of the dagger, his hand gripping tightly the well-worn leather hilt. It quickly dawned on me he too must have lost his balance during our brief struggle and fallen onto his own blade. There was nothing more I could do for him. But the girl! Where was she? I had, for a few moments, forgotten all about her. Yet she was the one who needed me the most. Taking a steady breath, I remembered seeing the guard throw the girl.

I stumbled wearily in the direction of the heap of splintered boxes. It did not take long to find her crippled form. Once again the cloak covered her face. I gently pulled back the hood. A quiet moan escaped her partially opened lips, and I immediately placed my arm around the base of her neck, trying my best to carefully lift her unconscious body away from the rotten refuse. Suddenly her moans turned to a sharp cry of pain. I gently I lowered her back to rest against the crates.

Looking down, I noticed a slim shard of wood, no longer than two inches, protruding from beneath her right breast. Gingerly touching it, I suddenly realised with horror that it had pierced straight through her fragile frame.

"Sir?" she sighed, so faintly that I barely heard her. "Sir?"

"Yes."

"Who … who are you?"

"My name is Anton, I'm a blacksmith," I whispered, as I gently brushed away a few loose strands of hair from her half closed eyes. "But hush now. Don't talk. I fear you're badly hurt."

"I'm scared. I ... I think I'm dying," she faulted in a barely audible murmur. Suddenly her body tensed as she overcame a short spasm of throaty coughs. Blood and saliva splattered against her cheek, staining her smooth lips.

"Please," I begged, holding her slim, delicate hand against my chest, "don't talk.

Save your strength. I'm going to try and get you some help."

"No! Please don't leave me. I don't want to die alone," she cried grasping my hand tighter.

"You're not—" a sudden lump in my throat stopped me from continuing. With effort I suppressed my emotion. "You're not going to die."

But as I looked into her eyes, I could already see that her soul was preparing to depart this world. Tears stung my eyes. This time I allowed them to fall as her fragile body rested against mine. "Why?" I whispered to myself.

For some reason, I felt such dread at the prospect of losing her. We knew nothing about each other, and yet there was some kind of belonging as I held her close.

"I'm so cold. Could … could you hold me, please?"

Brushing away tears, I rested my arm across her shoulders and covered her body with my own tattered cloak. It was not much, but it was the best I could offer her.

"Thank you," she whispered.

Gently, she lowered her head to rest upon my shoulder. As I began to caress her hair, her deep, tender eyes slowly closed as her last breath released itself from her sweet mouth. Cradling her still, slender figure, I gently lifted her, releasing her body from the vile thing that had stolen her life. Then, with her head hanging limply over my shoulder, I buried my face into the nape of her neck and prayed for her soul to find peace.

"Put her down!" demanded a voice behind me.

I turned and suddenly found myself facing a troop of city guards, all with their swords drawn.

"Help me—"

"I said put her down!"

I carefully lowered her body to the ground and raised my hands. Five of the guards rushed towards me and pushed me roughly up against the damp wall, pinning me with their weapons. Two of the blades pressed tight against the base of my neck, I could feel a trickle of blood run down my back. A sudden gasp to my left told me that they had discovered the dead guard.

"Captain Turell!" one of them shouted.

Immediately the rest of the guards ran to the prone body. A brief debate quickly ensued between them. Then everything went black. I was to realise later, one of the guards had hit me over the head with the pommel of his sword.

* * *

When I awoke, darkness blinded me, but as my eyes adjusted to the gloom, I soon realised I was being held prisoner in one of the cells at County Hall. I was to discover later the guard who died that fateful night was none other than the city's beloved Captain Turell. A man of noted honor, and one who had been decorated many times for his undying loyalty to the city and to the duke of our county.

Therefore, my beloved city had already deemed my guilt. It would be considered an insult to the memory of Captain Turell to even think of holding a trial in my defense, all the evidence they needed was there. One blood stained dagger, a beautiful young girl, found half-naked and now lying dead in the city cemetery. Her clothes ripped apart due to an attempted rape that had been foiled upon the arrival of their beloved captain, who then was murdered whilst protecting her innocence.

Within the day, I had been found guilty and condemned to swing by the neck until dead. Since then, I have been lying in this rat-infested cell, slowly counting my lonesome hours away.

* * *

A sudden screech from a darkened corner to my left causes my heart to skip a few beats awakening me from my memories. With annoyance, I throw a small stone into the darkness, striking something soft. A squeal emanates and a medium-sized rat runs out into the light. Before running off to the comfort of its home, it pauses and stares at me with its black orbs.

Leaning back, I try to soften the hard cold wall with a handful of two-day-old straw. It does not help much, but it is better than nothing. I then pull up a dirt-encrusted blanket to my unshaven chin and attempt to relax. To sleep seems absurd. I only have a few hours left, but sleep is the only comfort not denied me.

Listening to the soft scratching sounds of my companion as he goes about his own business, I feel drowsiness weave its lullaby spell upon me. My eyelids slowly turn to hundredweights, and I find that keeping them open is only making them heavier. Gently I allow myself to fall into the soft cloak of slumber.

* * *

I could only have slept a brief period of time when I'm aware that a bright light is slowly penetrating my eyelids. Instinct forces my eyes to open, but I keep them shut, as the light seems to shine bright enough to blind me. And so, covering them with the back of my hand, I carefully rise to face whoever it is that has entered my cell.

"Do not be afraid," a soft female voice whispers. "I mean you no harm."

"Wh … who are you?" I stammer. My mouth has gone dry. Although I know I should feel fear, I do not. Instead, I find myself feeling at peace. Warmth from her light begins to flow through my body, as whiskey does to a man who works the streets at night.

"Do you not know me?"

A sudden thought flashes through my mind, filling my soul with dread. "I'm not … I'm not dead, am I?"

Suddenly the whole cell fills with a magical sound of delicate laughter. Clear crystal notes cascade over my unprotected body like fine raindrops on a sunny day.

"Whatever made you think that?"

"You are not … an angel?"

A warm touch gently alights upon the hand that shields my eyes. A subtle scent of vanilla drifts across my face.

"Look at me," she whispers. The warmth of her sweet breath washes across my face, and my heart starts to beat faster.

I feel no pressure on my hand, and yet, it slowly lowers. Fear rules my mind. I clench my eyes tighter as the shade of my hand leaves my face.

"Look at me," she repeats. Her voice is closer. I can almost feel her soft lips brush against mine.

Never have I wanted to see something so badly. To open my eyes and bathe in her heavenly light—to touch her lips that are tormenting my senses so much and yet … they stay shut.

"Why can you not look at me?"

"I want to," I croak, "but …"

"You cannot," she continues. I nod nervously. There is a pause, and I can hear a slight movement in front of me.

"Do you fear the light?"

Before I can answer, her soft, warm lips gently caress mine in the briefest of kisses.

The suddenness causes my eyes to flicker open. As I feared, the light instantly blinds me, but slowly as I blink away my tears and become more accustomed to its glare, I find myself looking into the most beautiful pair of sky blue eyes I have ever seen. My heart flutters as I realise I have never seen such purity and innocence radiate with such power.

Gracefully she stands and glides to the center of my cell. Her gaze, never leaves my eyes, weaves me into her spell. I welcome it.

"Now do you know me?"

Tearing my eyes from her stare, my breath catches in my throat as my mind drinks in this vision before me. Clothed in a brilliant white flowing robe that radiates a light so bright and pure that I can actually feel its chastity, stands a young girl of ethereal beauty, the very same who had died in my arms only the other night.

Her long dark hair flows about her head as if she lies in unseen waters. Her movements so smooth and majestic, I have no trouble in believing that I can only be dreaming about this heavenly apparition. Her arms rise gently and she starts to drift back towards me. It is now, that I realise she does not walk, but floats above the ground. As she nears, I begin to edge away, unsure as to what will happen should she touch me. She stops. I see pain and disappointment crease her flawless face.

"Why do you fear me?" she asks.

At first my voice fails me as dryness constricts my throat. "You—you're a ghost!" I stammer.

She laughs lightly. "I am no more a ghost than you are dead."

Her words confuse me, and so I stop edging back.

"We belong together. You and me." She glides closer and her hand slowly strokes my face lovingly. "I have come to find you."

"Find me?"

She smiles, "Yes."

"But ... why? Why me?"

Any minute now I expect to be awakened from this extremely lucid dream by the sound of the gaoler's keys. But until then, I want this dream to continue because, for some reason, I feel I need to hear what she's about to say.

Looking deeply into my eyes, she takes me by the hand and starts to stroke my fingers softly. All the fear and pain that has been locked up within me since that fateful night, quietly soothes its way out of my body, through my hands and into hers. Her eyes reluctantly look away from me, releasing a bond that had momentarily connected us together.

"I am ... a sylph," she replies in a soft whisper.

At first I do not hear, her gentle touch has captivated all of my senses. Then slowly, as if forcing its way through a tangled bush, her words reach me.

"Wh … wh … what did you say?"

"My name is Jania, and I am a Sylph."

Now I'm convinced I am dreaming. The implication of what she's just said astounds me. I pull my hand away from her touch. "You are mocking me. Sylphs are faerie creatures from myths. Stories told to young children to help them sleep at night. If you are what you claim to be, how is it even possible?"

"In order for you to tell stories of mythical creatures, do you not need a belief in which to create them by?"

"I, I suppose so."

"We have always been here. Since the dawn of ages we have lived in harmony with you. You, nor any others of your race, can see our world, but we are there nonetheless. Occasionally one of our kind visits your world. I believe that this is the basis for your stories."

"If this is so, then why come looking for me, a simple blacksmith?"

She gently pulls back, contemplating her words carefully and gracefully kneels before me. "When the soul is created, it is created with a partner—a perfect companion.

"These souls are meant to be together but sometimes, somewhere along the web of time, they are separated and lost. For some, they learn to be content with this. They marry, raise children and yet, through out their lives, they are never truly happy, for they feel incomplete. They feel as if something is missing from their lives, but since they now have a family with responsibilities, they fool themselves into believing that this is their fate ... their destiny. For others, the feeling of being lost is so strong that they can never have a partner or marry. Instead they devote their lives looking for that special someone. Do you understand what I'm trying to say Anton?"

"I, I think so. I believe it is a feeling I have had for a long time. I have always wanted to leave my town and go in search of my destiny, but something has always held me back. I think you would call it fear. Fear of the unknown." Suddenly, for no apparent reason, my heart jumps and I am overcome with such hope and joy that any doubts I harbored regarding this dream are dashed. Like a jigsaw, pieces begin to fit together inside my head. Things that she has told me, feelings that have grown within me since that accursed night, they all begin to make sense. I take her by the hand and hold it close to my heart. "You came looking ... for me?"

She smiles and I see her eyes begin to moisten.

"You came because we share the same soul."

"No," she says, tears begin to slide down the side of her flawlessly smooth cheek.

I lean back, bewildered. "But you just said …"

"I came looking for you because I love you."

Hearing this ethereal beauty confess her true feelings towards me is more than I can take. I sit dumbfounded. Words leave me speechless, and all I can do is look at her exquisite features. Her long, delicate arms reach up to cup my face, her thumbs brush across my lips.

"Hold me, please," she whispers. "I have been searching for so long. Let me know that my quest is over."

Leaning forward, I gently place my hands upon her hips as she rises. I can feel the warmth of her body pulsate in steady rhythms. Her light grows brighter but its strength only heightens my emotions towards her. But as I look at my hands, I see how dirty they appear against her purity. Feeling sudden shame, I withdraw them.

"Hold me," she breathes.

"Jania, I'm dirty."

"Please."

I look into her pleading eyes. I can no longer hold back. Wrapping my arms around her slim waist, I hold her tightly against me.

* * *

Suddenly the door bursts open, and the light is immediately extinguished by darkness. At least, it is at first. A guard enters with a lit torch and the cell floods with a dirty light. I look desperately about trying to find Jania, but she is nowhere to be seen.

It was, as I feared, naught but a dream.

I hardly notice Father McGuire entering the cell holding the Holy Book in his hands, nor do I feel the two guards force me against the sullied wall to roughly snap a pair of rusting manacles across my wrists.

The dream felt so real. Her skin had been so soft and warm to the touch, her voice so musical and pleasing to the ear. I had dared to believe it to be true. Even now as I'm being pushed towards the door with the good Father McGuire in front, I look about me, desperately hoping to see any kind of evidence, anything to prove that Jania was more than a figment of my imagination. But nothing can be seen.

* * *

The cart is old and weak. It lumbers along the road. Although it's one of the main routes to the city walls, the cart still manages to find the occasional pothole, and I find myself being thrown against the bars like an old rag doll.

The crowds have come out in their hundreds to see me hang. I remember a time when it used to be me out there watching the guilty, cheering on the guards for their good work and throwing insults at the prisoners. I find myself wondering now, how many of them were actually innocent?

Father McGuire walks out in front, holding aloft the Holy Book, shouting out sacred psalms preparing my soul for the Lord's judgment. It doesn't bring me much comfort, knowing my innocence.

For reasons I've never been able to understand, the road to where the executions are held is a long one. Situated upon a hillside, overlooking the city stands an old oak tree that, according to local legend, has been there since the dawn of time. Left amongst the branches, swinging gently in the breeze, are the rotting corpses of the guilty, as it has been decided they do not deserve the decency of burial. Because of this, the area has earned the name "Heavy Tree."

Before I know it, the silhouette of the oak comes into my vision. Fresh victims still hang from its drooping limbs. City Guards, armed with pikes and pole arms, fight a losing battle as ravens proceed to eat from the lifeless carcasses.

As I near the site, I unwittingly catch sight of one of the carrion birds plucking out a lifeless eye. Its optic nerve, still attached, preventing it from leaving its owner. Frustrated, the bird flies off to find easier prey, leaving the released eyeball to hang uselessly down the side of the ruined cheek. Suddenly the body twitches and a groan escapes from its lips.

Dear sweet Jesus he still lives, I realise with horror. Is this the fate that awaits me? I have always believed death was instantaneous and that the offenders suffered no pain. Please, God, let my death be swift, you alone know of my innocence.

The cage abruptly comes to a stop, knocking me to my knees. My back jars. I close my eyes to fight back a sudden wave of nausea. But I am roughly pulled from my moment of concentration by an overly anxious guard.

Rotten tomatoes, bad eggs, and decaying cabbage are but a few of the objects thrown at me as I'm dragged towards a makeshift platform. Within feet from the cart, the guards and I are covered in a cloak of refuse and filth. The smell alone causes me to gag and I feel the nausea rush back with a force I fear this time I may not be able to control it.

A dirt-ridden guard pulls up alongside me. Leaning down from his horse he notices my discomfort.

"Throw up and I promise your death will be a slow and painful one. Understand?"

One look into his penetrating eyes tells me his threat is no idle one. Taking a deep breath, I desperately try to settle the violent urges that writhe and cavort within my stomach.

Suddenly the crowd parts and I find Heavy Tree towering over me. Father McGuire stands upon the makeshift platform, alongside him, a hooded executioner. A noose swings gently in the breeze.

As I begin to ascend the wooden steps, the crowds start chanting out even more abuse at me. Hearing all the hate and anger in their voices wounds me greatly, for I was once loved by many and had earned respect for my work. I know not what falsehoods the guards must have told, but they must have been great indeed to create a crowd such as this. Never in my born days have I seen so many from the city turn out for such an occasion.

"Fear not, for I am with you," whispers a voice from above the tumult of the people.

"Jania?"

I look about, but I see no sign of her.

The two guards that are supporting me up the steps look at me with puzzled faces.

"Did you not hear that voice?" I ask them.

"Keep your foul mouth shut!" snarls the closest.

The other laughs and cries out, "The only voice you'll hear will be from 'im downstairs as he devours your soul!"

"But you must have heard her?"

Suddenly the first guard grabs me by the throat. "Oi! I said shut it, you murdering bastard!"

"Brothers, please," cries out Father McGuire, "let us finish this distasteful work."

"Aye, Father," the guard mumbles. His grip, almost vice-like, lifts my neck higher, forcing me to go on tiptoes. "We should finish off this scum and quickly!"

"We wouldn't want anything to happen to him before he stretches now would we?" the second guard cackles.

Releasing his hold on me, I'm roughly thrown into the arms of the executioner.

"Would you be so kind as to lynch this piece of filth?"

Ignoring the guards' crude comments, the executioner silently takes hold of the noose and gently places it around my neck.

As I stand here, panic begins to seep its evil way into me. With the rope tightened against my throat, I realise with clarity that I am about to die. My last memory will be the sight of this hate-filled crowd, the smell of refuse and rotting carcasses and a feeling of utter loneliness.

"Please, you must release me!" I cry out. "I am innocent!"

"Save it for the other side boy," mutters the executioner.

"But I'm innocent I tell you!" I shout, but my voice is drowned out as the crowd's chant rises to a thunderous rapport.

"STRETCH! STRETCH! STRETCH!"

The executioner looks over to the newly appointed captain.

There is a pause, and I find my hopes briefly rise, solemnly the captain nods.

The hooded face turns to me, muttering a silent prayer, he then looks into my eyes and whispers, "Forgive me, Lord!"

His hand lowers to the wooden lever and grasps it firmly.

"NO!"

My voice is suddenly cut off as the trapdoor beneath me gives way. I hear a snapping noise come from inside and the lower half of my body instantly goes numb. I panic and try to force air through my throat, but I can't. My face starts to burn as I feel the blood pressure force its way into my head, my tongue shoots out, and the mounting pressure causes my eyes to bulge.

Darkness starts to cloak my vision, I hear the crowd's chant distort and turn to an uproar of cheers and applause as they watch my dangling body twitch in the early morning light.

* * *

Suddenly their cries of pleasure turn to screams of alarm. My eyes flicker open and I see their faces whiten with fear. The first couple of rows start to push back in panic. From behind, a slim pair of delicate arms lift me effortlessly. The noose falls loosely across my shoulders, and air forces its painful way into my desperate lungs.

The scent of vanilla drifts across my face and I notice a bright light begin to envelope my body. Looking about, I see the two guards stumble backwards into a shocked Father McGuire, their faces show pure terror. Even the hooded executioner collapses to his knees weeping.

The arms release me, and I realize I am still suspended above the open trapdoor. Carefully I lift the noose over my head and let it fall. My whole body is starting to glow with a life of its own. My legs tingle as I feel new life ebb its way into them.

"Now we can be together forever, Anton."

That voice, I recognise—and that smell of vanilla. Can it truly be? My heart beats violently against my ribcage as I dare to slowly turn and face Jania. Her inner light grows brighter as I feel my soul lighten with gladness at seeing that she had not forsaken me.

Her blue eyes penetrate deeply into my heart as I look into her innocent face. She looks even more beautiful now than she did the night before, if that was even possible?

"Am I still dreaming? Even now, as I die?"

"No," she smiles, "this is real. It is now time for me to take you home."

I looked down to realise I had begun to gently float upwards. Below, the frightened faces of the citizens stare up at us. I know now that I am different, for I am to leave this land of disease and poverty and enter a new one filled with hope and dreams of magic. Taking me there is the girl of my heart, my true love, Jania.

"Anton?"

Turning away from the pitiful sight of my past life, I gaze up at the eternal beauty of Jania, her arms open wide, her eyes tear-stained with joy.

"Shelter me with your love."

This time without hesitation, I let myself soar up into her arms. As we touch, the clouds before us part and a brilliant light floods over us and all those below. Smiling and with her hand in mine, Jania guides me through the opening and into another world of wondrous beauty. For I now realise I have finally awakened from a nightmare of despair to face a future of untold dreams. Who knows what is in store, but with Jania by my side, nothing can stand in our way.

THE FLIGHT

The Flight

Clouds, the colour of early twilight, part in their own aimless wanderings leaving the way forward open.

The lone figure, floating effortlessly upon the warm undercurrents, opens her arms wide, relishing the experience. Nothing can touch her here – everywhere is peaceful. Everything is beautiful. Even those clouds not fast enough to part only kiss the naked flesh of her body.

Looking above and below, she drinks in the beauty of this new world. There is no sun, only a rainbow of delicate blues to passionate reds.

As she wraps her arms tightly around her body, she finds herself flying faster, the gentle undercurrents turn into a warm caressing wind. Her long dark hair whips wildly about her as she twists her body downwards. Below she observes the land lying thousands of feet beneath her, showing off miles and miles of soft curves and contours.

There is so much freedom. She feels the need to soar down towards the earth to tease the ground with her touch. Twisting her body so that her back arches, she allows herself to drop out of the sky like a bullet. The wind shrieks past her ears, her hands tight against her thighs, the air turning slightly cooler as it rushes past her skin. She closes her eyes and feels the speed of her descent.

She is alive! Opening her eyes again, she sees the earth rushing towards her with finality, but she is in control and feels no fear. As the land screams closer, she suddenly pulls herself up and with a mighty roar in her ears, skims the land within mere feet. Her skin is aflame with sensation, and she can't hold back a small moan of ecstasy as it escapes her lips.

As she touches the earth with her fingers, she senses a presence hovering nearby. She pulls up from the ground and circles a tree, using the branches as cover. In the distance a silhouette alights upon a cloud and looks down at her. At first she is wary but she feels neither fear nor danger from this figure, in fact, as she watches it, she feels drawn to it.

It beckons her with its hand. She feels the need to be with it, though at this distance she still cannot see who or what it is. She feels no modesty as she leaves the protection of the tree. Whoever it is, she wants to be with it, the pull is too much, the need too great. Cautiously spreading out her arms, she rises with the warm undercurrents from the heat of the ground. The figure looms closer and she can make out that it is a boy with shoulder-length hair and a mischievous smile. Like her he is naked but for a small silver strand attached to his stomach that sails off into the distance.

She tries to talk to him but realises she is unable to speak. She touches her lips and they move. She can feel her tongue, why can't she speak? The boy laughs but no sound escapes his lips either. He floats down beside her and gently places his hand between her breasts. More from reaction than shock, she leaps back. His touch made her heart jump as if he were pure energy, but it felt good too, his hand was soft and it filled her with warmth. Slowly she floats back to him. His smile is becoming infectious as she finds herself smiling too.

Once again his hand reaches out to touch her. For a brief moment, she finds herself hoping his touch would become a caress. She blushes when his hand settles over her heart instead. She doesn't even know this boy or does she? Something about him feels familiar.

Suddenly she hears his voice in her mind; it seems to come to her as if on the wind, faint and airy.

"Hi. I've been waiting for you?"

She tries to answer him but fails. He takes her hand in his and places it upon his chest, just over his heart.

"Think your words. I'll hear them."

"Who, you? Like—should, you?" Although she tries to think her words, they won't come out clear.

"Close your eyes and feel with your hand, feel my soul. It's there in front of you, just reach out and touch it."

She closes her eyes. As she concentrates on her touch, she suddenly finds herself looking at a brilliant light before her. She quickly opens her eyes and sees the boy smiling back at her. His touch grows warm upon her.

"Reach out and touch it."

Once again she closes her eyes and looks upon the light, it appears to be in the shape of a heart but it shines with a brilliant white flame. It's so beautiful. Seeing her hand in her mind, she carefully touches his heart, or is it his soul?

Images and dreams suddenly flow out from his heart and into her, she catches a few scenes that show them together in another lifetime as lovers, she also sees a different time where they are forced apart. Are these dreams, images of what he wants her to see? Or did these things really happen? Some part of her feels that they actually did, at some lost and forgotten time. He feels so familiar, so safe.

Slowly the images fade, but if what she saw in them is true, then she and this boy have been partners throughout all time. Lovers in fact, they have shared their lives together in all incarnations. But why can't she remember?

She looks into the eyes of the boy and realises he has no pupils, his eyes glow with the same fire that encompasses his soul. She feels a strange sensation grow from where his hand rests. A tickling feeling builds, which can only be described as the feeling of butterflies from within. It radiates out from across her chest and down into her stomach. She's excited and cannot help but laugh. She lowers her head, allowing her hair to fall across her face as she shyly looks up at the boy, embarrassed as the tingling passes her stomach and settles between her thighs.

Her eyes close, the feeling gently intensifies.

"Who are you that I should feel these powerful emotions?" she whispers. Her hand, still touching his soul allows her question to be heard.

"I am your dreams. I am your passion. I am your spirit ... I am your love. Together we are one."

The boy releases his hold from her heart and with both hands, gently cups her face. His thumbs stroke her lips.

She looks back at him. His hands gently pull her to him. The boy kisses her tenderly. His lips are soft, warm, and inviting. His smell is intoxicating. She finds herself kissing him back, gently at first but then with a hunger. The kiss feels right and any doubt she has disappears. She wants him, she needs him.

Losing herself in the moment, she moves her arms around the boy's broad back. As her hands touch his skin, tiny sparks erupt from where they rest. There is a slight groan of pleasure from the boy as she gently pulls herself up, pressing her body against him.

Gentle flames envelope their skin, but they don't burn. He moves his right arm down her lower back and softly strokes her, his left hand cradles her head. Their legs entwine and the gentle tingling within her grows to an almost painful itch, painful, but pleasurable too. He breaks the kiss reluctantly, leaning his forehead against hers. She moves forward wishing to continue.

"Where are you?" he asks.

"What?"

"Where are you?"

"I'm here … with you." she replies, confusion etched across her face. She tries to lean in again.

"No, I mean where are you? I have been looking for you for so long, but I cannot find you."

She stops and notices tears appear from the corners of his eyes as they close.

"It has been so long since we last held each other," he whispers.

Understanding suddenly dawns upon her. She realises he has been looking for her in the real world. She also realises she needs to find him too. She smiles warmly at him.

"You found my soul. You will find me. You can make it happen."

White fiery orbs look back at her, and a ghost of a smile appears.

"Do you believe?" he asks.

The flames that surround them glow brighter. His body grows warmer, and the tickling sensation within her expands. She closes her eyes as the feeling is almost too much to bear. She sees his soul burning fiercely before her. She can feel its comforting warmth surround her. A beam of white fire slowly stretches forth from his soul towards her. She wants to touch it, but is afraid it will stop this intense feeling.

It caresses her and memories of him suddenly flood over her like a tidal wave. She finds herself remembering his smell, his touch, his presence, his magic. A love so powerful and pure, that only they could share. How could she have forgotten it all? She gasps as her feelings for him are awakened with intensity. Slowly she opens her eyes and she's aware they now cast a glow of their own, bathing his face in a gentle white light. He smiles back at her.

"Yes, I do!" she replies, her heart pounding with excitement.

She leans in to kiss him. This time he doesn't pull back. There is no gentleness, only the fierceness of long forgotten passion. He holds her tightly against her, almost crushing her. But she welcomes the pain, her own hands digging into his shoulders. They need each other so badly. She wraps her legs around him, pulling him closer. She can feel his body respond to her need, as his hands lower and cup her from below. His flames lick against her skin.

"I need you," they both utter breathlessly.

At first she feels a slight resistance, but her yearning quickly breaks that wall. She closes her eyes as she feels him enter her. The sensation that has been growing within her envelops him. She sees their souls touch. Waves of pure ecstasy course through her body, through both of their bodies. She cries out in pleasure wanting him to go deeper, her breath coming in short sweet gasps. They watch their souls start to merge. She opens her eyes and looks into his orbs.

"We are one," she whispers. She can feel everything that he is doing to her, every touch, stroke, and caress. He leans into kiss her, and she feels their bodies begin to merge.

"We truly are one," he answers.

The ecstasy within her screams to be released, but she tries to hold it back. She wants to treasure this feeling for as long as she can. She can feel him responding to her wishes, but it is a losing battle. The need is too strong.

They both let go at the same time …

* * *

The power of the release forces her awake. She finds herself caught up in her bed sheets. Her nakedness bathed in sweat, her heart hammering against her ribcage, her breath in short gasps.

It is still night.

What happened? Was it all but a dream?

Confusion descends upon her and she feels the harsh ache of loss. She quickly sits up and holds the sheet against her.

It was real! It had to be! She could remember every detail, his eyes, his touch, and his smell—his smell! She quickly pulls the sheets to her face and inhales. It can't have been a dream for she can still smell his sweat on her. Couldn't she?

She slowly lays back, doubt entering her mind like darkness. What happened? She has never had a dream as intense nor as real as that. It couldn't have been a dream. Slowly the room brightens as a small light appears in the air above the base of her bed, and she hears his voice inside her head.

"I will find you, for we will make it happen."

She smiles and his warmth comforts her as the light diminishes. It wasn't a dream. He will find her, but that's another story.

CHILD OF ALYKEÁ

Child of Alykeá

The shock wave threw him heavily into a clump of bushes as a tree nearby exploded from a lightning strike. He lay there for a second allowing his senses to realign. His vision was blurred from the sudden flash of light and his hearing was reduced to a high-pitched whine.

This storm was getting worse, and he could still see no end to the forest that surrounded him. Panic was starting to settle in, maybe there was no end. Hell, he thought, I don't even remember arriving here.

The rain lashed down on his upturned face as he tried to get back up onto his feet. The world tilted badly, and he had to lean heavily against another tree to regain his balance.

"Mathúin!" cried out a voice. It seemed to come from all around, as if from the storm itself.

He froze and looked about wildly. The trees were bending under the strength of the wind, the leaves, torn from the branches, were creating a maelstrom all around. Even the rain attacked him from all angles, making it nigh on impossible to keep the water out of his eyes.

"Mathúin!" the wind cried out again.

"What?" He shouted, but his voice was drowned out by the noise of the storm.

Suddenly realising that the tree he was leaning against could very well be the next target for the random lightning, he pushed himself away and tried to navigate through the surrounding undergrowth. Thorns and roots constantly tried to trip him up, but he persevered and forced his way through.

Minutes later, he became aware of a light off in the shadows. Hoping it could lead to some shelter, he started to make his way towards it. But the going became tougher as the fierce wind started to throw all kinds of debris across his vision, blocking his way, and forcing him to constantly cover his face for protection.

He soon realised no matter how much he fought the wind, the light stayed a constant distance from him. He couldn't seem to get any closer, but unwittingly it had become his sole purpose, he had to reach it. He didn't know why, but he knew safety lay within that light.

"Mathúin!" cried the voice once more. This time he was aware it wasn't the wind, but, in fact, the light. Or someone holding the light.

With a sudden need to be heard, he shouted out as loud as he could, "I'm coming! Wait!" But, as before, his voice was drowned out in the storm.

The light started to fade away. Suddenly his whole world lit up as another lightning bolt struck near him. The next thing he knew was darkness.

* * *

He opened his eyes and it took a few seconds before he realised that the sound of the wind was no longer with him, nor was the forest. In fact, he was in a warm bed, and as he looked around, it dawned on him that he was in his bedroom. He sat up and wiped his face, he was drenched in sweat and his heart was pounding like a bass drum.

It was only a dream, but what a dream! He tried to remember the details, but, as usual, the images were quick to fade. He looked over to his bedside cabinet and saw the digital display flash out 05:30. Too wired to even attempt to try and get back to sleep, he decided to get up instead.

Pulling back the covers he leaned out and switched on the bedside light. He then reached out, pulled open one of the drawers, and grabbed a small black book that sat inside.

He flipped it open and ran through the earlier entries he had previously written, occasionally stopping to read a small passage or two, until he finally came to an empty page. He then pulled out a small pen, hidden within the spine and started to write down all he could remember of his dream, adding small details as they came to him.

This was the third time this week that he had dreamt the same dream, and he found himself wondering whether there was something in it. Was there some kind of hidden message or was his body trying to tell him something?

For the umpteenth time, he found himself wishing he had asked Tanya more questions about why he should keep a dream diary and what some of these images could mean. For some reason she had thought it would be fun to compare dreams over their morning coffee at Frappo's before work.

He had never been able to get into that weird stuff she liked: the supernatural and the paranormal. But it seemed to please her, and, hell, he enjoyed being in her company. Although not a couple, he always played with the idea that one day they might end up together, they pretty much spent most of the time in each other's company anyway.

But now, that had all changed since she moved to London for a chance at promotion. Ironically, it was he who'd encouraged her to take the plunge in the first place, though he had never imagined that she would actually take it. She seemed so against the city, preferring instead the quiet life of the country. He obviously didn't know her that well, as it appeared she had taken to the city like a duck to water. Recently their phone calls had become quite short and business-like, and so he had resigned himself to the fact that he had lost her to the bright city lights.

He had planned on dropping the dream diary when she left, but for some reason he had found it therapeutic and sometimes quite helpful in understanding his own mental state. Through the diary he had come to realise that certain dreams occurred when he got stressed or if he was about to come down with something. It had become, for him, a kind of forecast to his immediate future, though he still looked upon all the other stuff as a load of nonsense, she hadn't convinced him quite yet. If he was truly honest with himself though, he would admit that he kept it because deep down inside, he hoped that Tanya would one day come back to him and that this diary was all that kept them connected.

Quickly brushing away these disturbing thoughts, he looked through some of the earlier entries again. This recent run of dreams had him concerned. He had found similar dreams scattered about in the past month. In fact, ever since his twenty-fifth birthday, they seemed to be increasing. Something was about to happen, though he had no clue as to what the dream portended.

Maybe I should try and call Tanya, he thought. *She may see something there I can't.* He looked back at the clock and quietly swore. It was still too early for breakfast. He quickly put the book down and stood up stretching.

After a moment, he said aloud, "Damn, I might as well go out for a jog." Even though he knew he was the only person there, it masked the loneliness he felt living alone. He briskly threw on loose jogging trousers, an old t-shirt and made his way out to the awakening world.

* * *

"Are you sure you didn't mistake it for your own name, Matthew?" Tanya asked.

"No. They—it definitely said Mathúin. I don't even know if it's a name or … or … a thing?" replied Matthew. "Do you know what it could be?"

"Not really, though it does sound Celtic. Give me a sec and I'll Google it."

Over the phone he could hear her typing frantically while he took another sip of coffee. He had been very nervous about calling Tanya, their last phone call was very brief, and he almost didn't recognise her as she had been quite short with him, though he had no idea why.

But this time was different, she almost sounded happy upon hearing his voice and after apologising for the way their last call ended, had started talking just like they used to in the good old days. She obviously wasn't very busy as they had been on the phone for about twenty minutes now, and she was still eager to talk. She had been very interested in his dream, as she claimed it held a lot of iconic references, almost too many. His initial hunch was right though, for she also suspected that something big was about to happen in his life.

Suddenly Tanya's voice broke through his thoughts "A-ha! Here we are!"

"What?"

"It's a Celtic name. It says here, that it's a shortened form of Mathghamhain, which means 'bear' in Irish Gaelic. Oh, Mathghamhain was the name of a brother of the Irish High King Brian Boru."

"Is that important?"

"No, not really, it's just a coincidence, I was reading a novel about Brian Boru the other day." She took a breath and then said, "You know, it does sound awfully similar to your name. Do you remember anyone ever calling you that when you were younger?"

He thought for a moment, but nothing came to mind "No, sorry. Why?"

She paused for a second before saying, "Well, I was just wondering what with your past being what it is ..."

He could tell straightaway she was unsure about how to broach him about his childhood. Other than his foster parents, she was the only other person who knew he'd been adopted. He had been found abandoned in the woods when he was about twelve years old, though they could never ascertain his actual age as he suffered from a serious case of amnesia. To this day, he still had no memory of his life before being found.

"What? You think that it may be my real name? That's stretching it a bit don't you think?"

"Yeah, maybe. But it wouldn't hurt to investigate your past? I mean, have you even tried?" she asked.

"Well, no. I was afraid I'd dig up something unpleasant. Also, truth be told, I didn't want to hurt my foster parents' feelings."

"Oh, okay. I can understand that. I just thought that, well, you know, now that you have your own place and all that you should think about it."

"Yeah, okay."

For some reason, an uncomfortable silence appeared and both were aware of it. Tanya was the first to try and break it.

"Hey, guess what? I'll be coming on down soon to see the old town again."

"Really?" Matthew tried to keep his tone normal, though inside his stomach was doing somersaults.

"Yeah, my little sister's getting married. I thought we could maybe catch up while I was there?"

"Hell, yeah. When is it?"

"In about two weeks time. the twenty-eighth I think. Will you be free? I thought maybe you'd like to come with me."

"Sure." He couldn't believe his luck. "You've got my mobile right? Well, call me when you get here."

"Of course—damn, the boss is on the prowl. Look, I've gotta go, if I don't call you before, I'll see you in two weeks time, alright? Ciao!"

"Yeah, ciao." And she hung up.

Wow, she was coming back for a weekend and wanted to spend it with him no less. He was on such a high that for the rest of the week he was floating. Nothing could bring him down, that is, until the dreams returned.

* * *

"Mathúin!"

The black clouds broiled angrily overhead as the storm's ferocity increased. Some of the smaller trees snapped under the pressure of the wind. Matthew desperately tried to find cover from all the carnage as the world about him erupted. No matter where he looked, he couldn't find the light through all the chaos, even though the voice was clear. He was also pretty sure it was a female calling out.

"Where are you?" he screamed.

One of the smaller trees caught him as it flew past, and he was knocked heavily to the ground, he needed to find shelter and fast. He was suddenly aware of his shadow to his left, and, turning to the right, he saw the light no farther than fifty feet away from him.

"Mathúin!" it cried out again.

Yep, it was definitely female he thought to himself as he attempted to get up, but the storm was doing it's hardest to pin him down by throwing everything at him.

"Don't go! Please, I'm coming!" he shouted, but part of it got muffled as a fistful of dead leaves got blown into his mouth.

"God damn it!" he screamed to himself. "I shall not be beaten by a bit of wind!"

Spitting out the leaves, he forced his legs beneath him and crouched into the tempest. Then slowly, using his arms to push the debris aside, he staggered his way towards the light.

It was painful work, and his exposed skin was constantly being ripped opened by the lashing thorns, but he was making headway. The light couldn't have been more than twenty feet away, when he thought he could make out a figure holding a lantern.

Then, as before, a lightning bolt struck nearby, and he was showered in rubble. He quickly brought his arms over to protect his head and buried his face into the forest loam … and woke up sweating.

* * *

That morning, whilst at work, Matthew did a quick Google search for the forest he had been found in. Not much came up, but he did find an address of an old boarding school that was based in the centre of the woodland. He jotted this down along with the telephone number then printed off a few maps of the area. Without realising it, he had already resigned himself to visiting the place as soon as possible.

It was too far to go after work, and so he decided to go over at the weekend. But then he realised he was supposed to meet Tanya for the wedding. Oh well, that takes precedence, he thought, I'll go on Sunday. Hell, you never know, maybe Tanya will want to come along for the ride.

He then decided to do a few searches for the name of Mathúin, but these also didn't provide much, other than the usual sites for the meaning of names and a brief history of King Brian Boru. A dead-end basically, none of it useful.

The dream was now visiting him on a nightly basis. Each time he dreamt he was getting a little bit closer to the light. By the time the weekend arrived, he was almost desperate to visit both the forest and the boarding school. They were definitely calling out to him. Though he didn't know why, he knew, without a doubt, he'd find all the answers there. He'd even tried to call the boarding school, but the number came up as disconnected. No doubt closed down, another ruin rotting away.

The whole mystery was deepening, Matthew became almost obsessed with the whole thing, and he noticed his work was starting to suffer because of it. He found he was constantly replaying the scenes of the dream in his mind. Who did the voice belong to? Why were they calling out that old Celtic name? And why was he dreaming the same dream every single night?

Saturday finally arrived and yet he was still surprised when Tanya called his mobile phone. Somehow, over the week, the dream had become more of a priority than spending time with Tanya. He was surprised to find a part of him resenting her call, as he had decided to visit the forest early Saturday. But he had already promised he'd go and when he drove over to collect her, he was glad he had. She looked absolutely stunning in a dress of deep royal blue, which shimmered when she walked, and he found all his emotions about her wash over him again.

Even though they had only spoken the other week, it felt weird seeing each other again. On the drive to the church, their conversation was a bit stilted. It felt as if they both wanted to say something, yet were too afraid to say it.

The wedding itself went without a hitch. The sun was out. There wasn't a cloud in the sky. Everyone had a great time and for those few hours, Matthew finally felt as if he and Tanya had become an item. They touched, held hands, and laughed together as the photographer tore out his hair trying to organise the children for the family shots. He was even asked to be included in some of the photos, standing proudly next to Tanya.

It was an amazing day and as the sun set. Matthew and Tanya found themselves huddled in the corner of the marquee reminiscing about the things they used to get up to at work. After a particularly violent fit of giggles had died down, the result of a story from Matthew about an embarrassing office prank that had disastrously backfired, Tanya finally asked him about his dream. She instantly regretted it, as the light in his eyes diminished, and his smile suddenly turned sullen.

Seeing the drastic change, she immediately apologised, "I'm sorry Matthew, I didn't mean to be a killjoy."

"No, no, it's alright," he said. "It's just that I've had the dream constantly this past week now, and today is the first time I've finally been able to think of something else."

He looked at her. "I was becoming obsessed with it, desperate to find out what it meant. I think I've finally found somewhere I can find the answers. And, you were right. I think it's got something to do with my past. I need to return to the forest where I was found."

Smiling, Tanya took his hand in hers and said, "Really? Well that's wonderful, isn't it?"

"Yeah, well, it was. Now that I've come up for air, so to speak, I'm nervous about what I might find."

"But this could be important?"

He laughed and looked across the room at the dancers. "Ha! Tell me about it. I've got this real strong feeling, that whatever I find, will forever change my life."

He looked back at her. "You know, I've put some serious thought into your idea."

"Which one was that?"

"About my name, I'm starting to think it could be this Mathúin. But who the hell would call their kid such an archaic name?" He paused for a moment, taking a sip from the champagne they were sharing.

"I was told they gave me my name 'Matthew' because it was the only word I spoke when they found me. At least, that's what they thought I said. What if I was saying this other name?"

"Well then, we'd just have one more clue towards solving the mystery of Matthew Donaghan then, wouldn't we?" she smiled. He couldn't help but smile with her.

"You make it sound as if I could be some kind of forgotten royalty."

"You never know, stranger things have happened. If you are, I want to make sure you don't forget about those that care for you. Like me for instance."

"Ha! Says she who ran away to the big city, leaving me behind, all alone to fend for myself."

She raised her hand mockingly. "Hey, I'd have you know, mister, that the opportunity arose, and I took it. Hell, if I remember correctly, you even encouraged me! I thought you were trying to get rid of me."

Laughing, he replied, "You were supposed to read between the lines and realise I was hoping you'd stay! Who else have I got to share my early morning coffee with?"

It was her turn to look melancholy now. "Yeah, well, you know what? I wish I hadn't left. I never realised how much I enjoyed my time here."

"But I thought you loved London?" he asked her bewildered.

"I did at first, but I soon came to realise all I had become was another number in the system. I'm losing my identity. Nobody really cares about what I think or what I believe— and the stress! My God, don't even get me started on that one. Everything has to be done yesterday. No, the more I think about it, the more I want to come back."

She took the glass from him and sipped it. "I know we still get stressed out down here, but somehow with all this beauty around us, the woods, the moors. It just never seemed that bad. Plus—" she looked at him coyly, with the hint of a smile, "you made everything fun."

Matthew was stunned, he didn't know if it was the champagne talking or what, but was Tanya hitting on him? Or was she just playing with him again? "I, I did?" he stammered.

"Of course, you were always there to cheer me up, to make me feel special. I just didn't realise how special, until I hit the big city." She moved closer to him and his heart started thumping as if he was running a hundred-yard sprint.

"Why didn't you tell me to stay?" she asked. Although he could smell the champagne on her breath, her eyes were quite clear.

"Because, um," but he couldn't voice the real reason, his mind was in overdrive. He was afraid he was going to say something stupid.

"Matthew, I've known you for what? Five years now? I can read you like a book. Why didn't you ever make a move on me?"

She was even closer now, their noses almost touching.

"I, I thought you only saw me as a friend, I didn't …" but he was cut off as Tanya leaned in and kissed him.

It was as if a dam had burst within. Now that he knew Tanya felt the same way towards him as he did her, he didn't hold back. He returned her kiss with equal passion. It seemed the whole world stopped for the two of them.

"It's about bloody time!" said a cheerful voice to their left, breaking the spell.

They quickly pulled apart to see Tanya's sister and her new husband looking down at them smiling.

"You two have been mooning for each other long enough." Tanya's sister smiled. "I'm just glad it happened on our wedding day. Now we can say with confidence, this day has been perfect!" Then grabbing her husband's hand, she turned to leave.

"Congratulations," he laughed out as he was dragged away.

Both Matthew and Tanya looked at each other and blushed. They both felt like a couple of young teenagers who had been caught doing something guilty. But then they shared a laugh and carried on from where they had been interrupted.

* * *

"Matthew!"

The dream evaporated as he forced his eyes open. The bedside light was on. His digital clock read 04:07. He was aching and soaked in sweat.

"Matthew?"

He turned over and saw Tanya laying next to him, naked, a concerned look etched across her face. "You were having the dream again," she stated.

He sat up, wiping his face dry. It was all so vivid; every detail had stayed with him.

He turned to her. "I've got to get to the forest."

"Why?"

"I don't know, but the dream was different this time. Usually it fades when I wake up, but now I can remember everything, as if I was still there." He turned away. "God, what is happening to me?"

She sat up and draped an arm around him. Placing a tender kiss on his shoulder she asked, "What changed this time? Tell me what happened."

He took a moment to catch his breath. "It, um, started the usual way: being lost in the forest, the hurricane winds, the voice crying out with a light in the distance and, as usual, I started to make my way towards it. All the while, the storm is using the forest to try and stop me. Each time I find myself fighting against it.

"Well lately, I've been able to get closer and closer each time. But tonight, I finally did it. I reached the light." Looking off into the distance, he whispered to himself, "I finally reached it."

"And?" asked Tanya impatiently.

He looked back at her. "Oh … um … well, all of a sudden the winds died, and I found myself standing in sunlight. There wasn't a trace of the storm anywhere and in front of me were all these people. But they weren't like you and me. They were dressed in, in, well, the only way I could describe it, was that it, it looked like they were wearing leaves of some kind. But beautifully made, they didn't look fragile or anything and their faces, their faces …" once again he seemed to drift off.

After a couple of seconds waiting, Tanya gently shook him, and his eyes focused back on her "Sorry," he apologised, "it's just that it's all so vivid to me. It's amazing! I can still see everything."

"What did these people look like, Matthew?"

"Their, um, their faces were so beautiful, so fragile, as, as if they were made from porcelain. They almost didn't look human, you know, like those fairy statues you can buy, but they were the same height as us, and, and their movements were so graceful. One of the women came up to me, and she was smiling as if she knew me. She reached out to touch me and said. 'Mathúin, thank the spirits that you have finally heard our call. It has been so long. Please, it is very important you come back to us, before it is too late.'"

"And you know what the weird thing was? I felt that I should know her. In fact, I felt I should know all of them, But then the winds started to come back and the light dimmed, and something was happening to me, something terrible. It felt like I was being ripped in two. I could feel my skin tearing apart, and all I could do was scream. And that must be when you woke me, because the next thing I saw was—was you."

It suddenly dawned on Matthew where he was and who was sitting next to him. He looked at her with new eyes, drinking in her nakedness and smiled, the dream fading away like mist. This was the dream he had wanted to come true for so long. He slowly reached out and stroked her face.

"My God, you are so beautiful. I … I can't believe you're here, next to me. What happened?"

Closing her eyes, she nudged his stroking palm and smiled. "I don't know, but it feels so good."

With his thumb stroking her cheek, he gently raised her face and leaned in, slowly kissing her lips.

"Do you have to go to the forest now?" she asked when he pulled away.

"Well, not right now. Why?"

She giggled and tenderly kissed him back. "Matthew, you are so blind sometimes. We have got some serious catching up to do. Then, and only then, will 'we' go to the forest."

"We?"

"Yes, we, you idiot! Now shut up and kiss me!"

* * *

They'd been driving non-stop for two hours, when the forest finally appeared on the horizon. The early morning sun had disappeared about an hour ago. Low cloud coverage now turned the world a dark murky grey.

Matthew pulled over in a lay-by to examine the old maps he had printed out in more detail. It seemed the entrance to the boarding school wasn't too far away from where they'd parked. He was starting to get nervous, and he could tell that Tanya was too.

That morning had been amazing; he still couldn't believe they were together. He had almost expected this to be the dream and the other, the reality. As he looked across at her, he couldn't help but replay the events that had lead to last night's adventure.

He had originally planned to drop her off at her family's house, but she obviously had different ideas. He parked outside her house with the engine running, but when he leaned over to kiss her good night, it all suddenly became a bit serious. No longer were they content with a simple good night kiss.

She whispered in his ear that she wanted to go back to his place, and he obliged, not that he needed much encouragement. What followed was better than anything he could have ever imagined. She was the most beautiful thing that ever happened to his life.

"You okay?" he asked.

"Yeah. I'm fine. I've just, um …" she fiddled with one of the print-outs. "I've got this weird feeling."

"What? About us?"

"Oh God, no. No, it's to do with …" she held up the map and pointed out towards the forest "—this. What we might to find."

"Yeah, I know what you mean," he looked out to where she had pointed. "Part of me wants to turn round and go back to the bedroom." She giggled and he smiled with her. "But I know that I've got to do this, and the longer I leave it, the worse it'll get."

"Hey, ignore me. I'm just being silly. It's an adventure, and I'm glad that it's one that we can both share," she said.

He leaned across and kissed her. "Hell, there may not be anything here anyway. Don't forget, this is all from a dream I had. I could just as easily be losing it from too much caffeine, or maybe I'm a secret midnight cheese-eater."

She laughed and the atmosphere lightened in the surrounding gloom. "Come on, let's get this over with. Show me the entrance, toots," he said with a bad Bogart impersonation.

"Toots?"

He laughed at her expression and pulled out onto the open road.

* * *

As they'd surmised, the turn off wasn't that far away, and his earlier assumption that the school had been abandoned was confirmed by the bad state of repair the road was in. In fact, it was more of a dirt track. He had to slow down to avoid the more serious potholes.

"Lucky thing, not bringing the Ferrari," mocked Tanya as they hit a particular nasty hole.

Matthew didn't reply, he'd just bitten his tongue.

The dirt track went on for about a mile before opening up into a wide forecourt. Before them, standing all forlorn and forgotten was the old boarding school. Three stories of crumbling bricks, mortar, and boarded up windows looked down upon the slowly advancing car. Matthew pulled up alongside a couple of wide steps that led up to a huge pair of oak paneled doors under a grand porch supported by two large ribbed columns. Warily, they looked at each other before exiting the car. The encroaching trees that flanked the old forecourt muffled the sound of the doors closing. Everything was grey and dying.

"Do you think anyone's home?" Matthew joked, but all he received was a faint smile. The whole place felt … wrong.

Tanya slowly walked up the steps to the doors. "Matthew, is this where you were?"

"Yeah. I vaguely remember being here, albeit briefly. I think this is where they brought me when I was found."

He noticed that Tanya had placed her hand on one of the doorknobs. "Is it locked?"

"Afraid so," she gave the handle a jiggle. "I can't seem to—"

CRACK

She instinctively jumped back, as the old door ominously swung open on rusted hinges, the sound echoing through out the building like an old fifties horror movie.

Concerned, Tanya looked down at Matthew as he made his way up to her. "Do you think we should go in?" she asked.

"Well, we're here now. As long as we're careful, we should be okay."

Taking a farther step away from the doorway, she allowed Matthew to enter first.

Inside was dark and smelt of damp and rot. All furniture and fixtures had either been taken or torn out. The place was a complete ruin. In the distance, reaching further into the gloom stood the grand staircase. The only light illuminating the entrance came from the open doorway, their shadows stretching across the foyer. Darkness seemed to suffocate everything.

Matthew looked back at the silhouette of Tanya as she stood on the threshold of the doorway. "You, um, didn't happen to bring a torch with you, did you?"

"No, sorry," she mumbled.

She gazed around wide-eyed and then peered at Matthew. "Do you feel anything?"

"A looseness of the bowels …" Tanya laughed, but it didn't break the mood, and she quickly quieted.

Matthew noticed a few doors on either side of the foyer and decided to try them but they were either locked or had swollen shut. Looking around, he was able to make out where the receptionist's desk had once stood as the tiles had been cut around the base and all that was left was a shallow hole.

This left him without many options. He found himself glancing up at the old staircase. He looked back at Tanya. She'd ventured farther into the foyer but hadn't left the trail of light. "Hey, sweetheart, you'd best stay near the door, just in case we've got to get out quick. I'm going upstairs."

"You sure?" she sounded concerned and he didn't blame her, he wasn't too happy about it either.

"Not really." He reached into his jacket and pulled out his mobile phone to use as a torch. "Don't worry. If anything jumps out, I'll be sure to get a good photograph of it."

"Just be careful."

Flicking on the light he was surprised at how bright it was. "No excuse now," Matthew whispered to himself and so, taking a deep breath, stepped on to the first step and was relieved to feel solid stone under the soiled carpet. Emboldened, he quickly made his way up to the first landing where he was given the choice of taking either the left hand set of stairs or the right hand set.

He chose the left, but was more cautious this time. The light from below had disappeared. He found he had to rely purely on the phone. It didn't help inspire confidence as it bathed everything in a sickly white light and had an annoying habit of switching off every thirty seconds.

The stairs soon ended. He found himself looking down a long corridor with a number of closed doors on either side.

"Tanya?" he shouted.

"Yeah?" she replied, a little bit too quickly.

"Er … nothing, just checking," he coughed. "You, um, wouldn't think any less of me if I started to scream like a little girl, would you?"

"Why? Are you?"

"Not yet, but it's very dark up here, and, um, really, really creepy."

He spent a moment looking about then decided to check the second door on his left. He had no idea why, it just felt right. The door appeared dry and with a quick twist of the handle, it swung open easily. The room inside was quite big, but as with everything else, appeared empty except for a hole where the fireplace once stood. Still, Matthew decided to enter. He seemed to remember something about this location, but couldn't quite put his finger on it.

Suddenly the light went out and he was plunged into total darkness. He cursed and pressed the keypad expecting the usual illumination from the screen, but nothing happened.

"Aw, crap!"

The sudden noise of something large shifting immediately grabbed his attention. He froze. Something was in this room with him. It moved again. He started to hit the keypad frantically, but it stayed dead. Hastily, he edged back, towards where he assumed the doorway was, his right hand waving erratically, desperate to find the handle.

"Mathúin! Get out!"

The voice was from his dream and had come from the far side of the room, away from the shifting noise, somewhere near the windows. His hand touched something solid and he groaned with relief when he recognised it as the door handle. He quickly stepped out of the room and slammed the door shut. A sudden white light momentarily blinded Matthew. He screamed. He then realised it was his phone and suddenly felt foolish.

"Matthew?" Tanya's voice came from below. She sounded worried now. He knew she would be coming up the stairs any minute.

"Go outside, Tanya! I'm coming down!"

"What is it?"

He ignored her for a second as he hurried towards the stairs and started making his way down. "Erm, nothing … just meet me outside."

He heard the door behind him shudder as something heavy fell against it. He stopped, turned, and in the ghostly light, saw the frame crack as something threw itself against the door a second time.

"Aw, crap!" he swore.

"Hurry, Mathúin!" cried the voice. It seemed to come from everywhere, just like it did in his dream.

He immediately decided to throw caution to the wind and sprinted down the stairs.

"Matthew?" Tanya was at the bottom of the stairs, her hand on the railing.

"Outside! Now!" he shouted as he rounded the landing.

Surprised at seeing Matthew hurtling down towards her, Tanya momentarily froze before spinning on the spot and running for the door. By the time she reached it Matthew was right behind her. They didn't stop until they were crouching behind the far side of the car.

"Matthew, what was that voice?" Tanya finally asked as they peered over the bonnet.

He turned to face her, shocked. "You heard it too?"

"Of course, it was everywhere. It—it told you to hurry!"

He looked back at the doorway and quietly swore to himself, "Then I'm not going insane."

"Who was it? Why were you running?" she asked.

He kept his eyes on the door "There was something in there, with me. As to the voice? I have no idea, but I'm sure it was the same one I dreamt about." He glanced at her nervously "I, er, decided to do as it suggested."

"Sound advice."

It was then they realised it was raining.

Looking up at the clouds, Matthew wiped the water from his eyes, "Aw, screw this," he uttered. "Let's just get out of here and go home."

"But, what about?"

"It's nothing Tanya, it was just a dream. Let's just leave it at that."

Tanya agreed, but she didn't move to the other side of the car, the passenger side next to the oak-paneled doors. Matthew noticed this and said, "You can get in from this side if you want." She smiled as if embarrassed, but still took him up on his offer.

As soon as she sat down, she locked her side and he followed suit. He then turned the key, but nothing happened. No click, no chug, no nothing.

"Aw, come on! You have got to be kidding me!" cried Matthew.

"Don't tell me we're out of petrol."

"Nope, we've still got half a tank. The car's just not starting."

"Well, at least we've got our mobile phones." She smiled as she held up hers.

"Something tells me that there's not going to be a signal," he muttered to himself. His suspicion was confirmed when she swore.

"Ok, I'm going to have a quick look at the engine," he said as he reached under the steering wheel and pulled a lever. "I'll be back in a sec."

The rain was now coming down in torrents. Matthew pulled his jacket up over his head, not that it made any difference. He fumbled under the bonnet for a few seconds before releasing the catch and swung the bonnet up. He didn't know much about engines, but he'd been able to pick up a few tips from friends. After doing a few cursory checks, he realised the engine was fine, as far as he could tell. He slammed the hood shut and hurried back into the car.

"Perfect," he said as he closed the door and pulled his jacket tight around him. "I couldn't see anything wrong with the engine, nothing, nada! It's like we're stuck in some damn Stephen King novel." He looked around and then sighed, "Hey, sweetheart, you still got the maps there?"

Tanya opened the glove compartment and pulled out the dog-eared printouts. "Yeah, here they are."

He took them from her and quickly looked them over. He then sighed as he closed his eyes "I don't believe that I'm going to suggest this, but there's appears to be a house near here ... God we 'are' stuck in a bloody novel!"

"But didn't you say that this was the only building in these woods."

"Yeah, I know. I must have over looked it ... but see here, on this ordnance survey map? There appears to be a small building about half a mile away. It didn't appear on any of the others, as I was only interested in the road maps. I just wanted to know where the forest was and how to get here." He looked over to her "What do you think?"

She smiled and said "All the movies would suggest that this is where the homicidal murderer would live but this isn't a movie and we need to get help I say let's go."

He smiled at her "You know? That's why I love you so." and he leaned over and kissed her. "Do you still want to come out from this side?"

She looked back at the school and at the darkened doorway that yawned at her from only a few feet away "Of course I bloody well do!" she said as she clambered over the gear stick "Move over!"

As Matthew slammed the car door shut, he was suddenly aware of a crashing sound coming from inside the school. He chanced a quick look at the entranceway and heard something break free.

Luckily Tanya hadn't noticed, so instead of alarming her, he grabbed her hand and sprinted across the forecourt to the nearby trees, where they managed to find some shelter from the downpour.

Tanya looked around, the rain clouds and tree cover had swallowed most of the light and she found her vision heavily restricted "Which way?"

"Erm. This way, I think." pointed Matthew.

He had realised to use the maps in this rain would be useless, so he had tried to memorise the direction of the building in relation to where the school was. He just hoped his sense of direction was good enough.

* * *

After about ten minutes of trawling through undergrowth and thorn bushes, they finally came upon an old animal trail that made travel a lot easier. Although the rain hadn't let up, it was the wind that started to cause them problems. Debris and loose branches were constantly being caught on their clothes, slowing them down considerably.

Tanya stopped for the third time in as many minutes to untangle herself from another thorn bush when they both heard an almighty crash come from the direction of the school.

"What the hell was that?" she cried out.

Matthew, who had stopped to help her, looked off into the distance.

"I think it was a tree falling!" he shouted back. The wind was definitely picking up.

"I don't think the wind's that powerful!" she shouted back.

"It's not! I, er I think it was pushed!"

Startled, she looked at him.

"Tanya, I think we're being followed!" He admitted, "From the school!"

"What?"

"Something was in that school I heard it break free and, um and I think it's after me. That's why the voice told me to run!"

"But nobody can push a tree over!"

Grabbing hold of the snagged branches, Matthew ripped them loose. "Tanya, I, I don't think we're in the real world anymore," he avoided her eyes. "I think that we've, we somehow, entered my dream!"

She looked at him as if he had finally lost it. "Please, Matthew. Don't say that!"

Instead of answering, he grabbed her hand and started to run, but she resisted. "No, Matthew! Tell me what's going on!"

He turned to look at her. How could he explain what he didn't understand? He was going on pure instinct, he knew whatever was behind them was very, very dangerous and they had to get away from it at all costs.

"Mathúin!"

Tanya, stunned, looked at Matthew and said, "Did you hear?"

He closed his mouth, held up his hand and instinctively looked around. There, off in the distance, Matthew saw the familiar light. Behind, he could clearly make out the sound of something large forcing its way towards them.

He grabbed Tanya by the shoulders. "Please, trust me on this. You must follow me!"

She didn't understand how this could have possibly turned from a simple excursion, into his nightmare, but she trusted Matthew. She nodded and allowed him to lead her away from the sound of snapping trees. It was then she also noticed the light that Matthew was heading for. Could it be? She thought.

As he'd described in his dream, moving forward became harder and harder.

In the blink of an eye, the wind had become a ferocious beast and they found themselves having to lean into it at impossible angles, just to make headway. Bushes and small trees were being uprooted and hurled at them, but this time, instead of lightning attacking from above, they could hear something huge slowly advancing on them. She wanted to turn and see what it was, but fear kept her fighting forward.

Matthew had become an unstoppable machine. It was as if his dreams had trained him for this moment. Whatever came his way, he was able to easily avoid or maneuver his way around it. He often looked back to check that she was okay, and she realised she was holding him back.

"Mathúin!" the voice cried out again.

Tanya was amazed, what with the screaming of the hurricane winds and the explosions of the following … thing, this voice could still sound so clear. It was a beautiful sound, and she could partially understand Matthew's need to follow it.

* * *

Matthew, on the other hand, now felt the full power of the voice. He could feel freedom ahead, his very core screamed out at him to hurry up and reach the light. The obstacles that were thrown his way were easily manageable and he felt an excitement build within him. I'm coming home!

He looked back and noticed a strikingly beautiful girl desperately trying to keep up with him. A part of him remembered her, but the call was too strong. Even so, he couldn't help but drop back and let her catch up. He knew her from somewhere and so reached out to take her hand. The minute they touched, everything came back in a sudden rush.

"Tanya?"

"I'm sorry. I'm trying, but the wind is too strong!" she screamed.

"No! I, I—" How could he explain that for a few brief moments he had become someone else, someone who didn't know her or what she meant to him. "Use me as support!" he rectified.

She smiled "My gallant warrior!" then grabbing his arm, pulled herself up into his embrace.

Looking over her shoulder, he could see the Guardian smash its way towards them relentlessly. He stopped himself, Guardian? How did he know that it was called this? He couldn't, but at the same time he did. His mind suddenly exploded with images of another life, a life of someone else. He cried out as he felt himself going through a mental shut down.

Tanya caught him as his legs buckled. "Matthew?" she cried "What's wrong? What's happening?"

He took a steadying breath and managed to control the images. He glanced at Tanya and tried to smile. "I'm okay, just a headache. Look, we've got to get to the light, before that, that thing gets here! Please don't ask me how I know, I just do."

"I know, I, I think I'm starting to understand. Come on, it's not far!"

With her arm wrapped round him, Tanya managed to help him stand. He felt strength flow through him again. He thanked her with a brief kiss and then, grabbing her hand tightly, as if too afraid to lose her, he pushed on, fighting his way through the flying debris. Every second felt like an hour, each foot of ground became a mountain to conquer, but together they savagely fought on. Behind, the Guardian slowly gained on them, its tread causing the ground to shake with each footstep.

The light was only about ten feet away when suddenly they heard an intense tearing sound come from it. They looked up and saw what they could only describe as the very air itself tear apart as if it were material. Soon it was big enough for the both of them to pass through, its light spilling out upon the ground all around.

"Matthew?" Tanya gasped as she stumbled in shock.

She couldn't believe what she was seeing. The light wasn't a lantern or light source of any kind, but in fact an opening: a portal from this world to another. Beyond, she could just make out majestic mountains and a cloudless sky with a large sun. She could even feel its heat beating down on her.

"Don't stop, Tanya! Keep going!" shouted Matthew.

"Be not afraid, child." the voice said kindly, and she found that she could make out figures standing near the entrance.

Behind, the creature suddenly let loose a bellowing roar of frustration and she quickly decided that whatever was beyond was by far better than what lay behind.

She tightened her grip on Matthew's hand, took a deep breath, and threw herself through the opening. She landed heavily onto lush grass. She heard Matthew land next to her with a grunt.

She lay there for a moment, trying to catch her breath. Everything was still, the sun was warm on her back and birds sang their chorus around her. The storm she and

Matthew had fought their way through, no longer existed. It was almost like waking up from a dream.

She quickly sat up. "The creature!"

"Tanya, it's okay," said Matthew breathlessly beside her. "It's a Guardian and therefore can't pass through." She looked over at him.

"How can you know that?"

His face was scratched and bleeding, his hair tussled. But there was something different about him. His eyes, he looked … wiser.

"Matthew?"

He shook his head and smiled a sad smile. "No, not anymore. Your original guess was right. My name is Mathúin, and I'm starting to remember … things. But a lot of it's still hazy."

"It will come back, in time," said a female voice off to the side.

Tanya saw him look behind her and smile. He then carefully got to his feet before reaching down to help her stand.

She quickly brushed herself down before looking around. She had once visited Switzerland and that was the only way she could describe her surroundings. The mountains she glimpsed earlier towered over them formidably, and all around were verdant pastures with a small sleepy village nestled down in the valley next to a sparkling blue lake. The buildings were simple and made of wood. They looked rustic, but felt homely. Smoke lazily climbed from small chimneys into the skies. No roads could be seen, no electrical pilings, just nature in all her glory. In fact she felt completely cut off from any form of technology.

Surrounding them, were about thirty people of various ages, all extremely beautiful and graceful, with finely etched faces and creamy complexions. They were dressed exactly as Matthew had described in his dream, in some material that resembled leaves. The men were clothed in only trousers, while the women wore simple slips that ended mid thigh. Some were in autumn colours, others in spring. If she believed in fairies, this is what she imagined that they would look like, only these were taller.

Tanya then turned to face the young woman whose voice had guided them here. If she thought the others were beautiful, this one was angelic. Her hair was long and seemed to be made of the purest silver, her eyes were the colour of violets and her smile made Tanya nearly weep in awe. Although her clothing was no different than the others, she felt more regal; she was the leader here.

Tanya couldn't help but fall to her knees in this young woman's presence.

She was suddenly ashamed of how she must look in front of these people, she felt dirty and imperfect. Matthew's hand rested upon her shoulder, and he knelt down next to her.

"Tanya?"

She turned to him. He didn't seem fazed by any of this. His manner was comfortable as if he had come home.

"Where are we? Is this where you are from?"

He smiled and replied, "I'm not too sure, but yes, I believe that this is … my home."

"Mathúin, come to me my, love," said the young woman, her arms open wide. "It's been so long."

He briefly kissed Tanya before walking over to this woman. He hesitated, but then fell into her arms and hugged her tight. Tanya's heart tinged in jealousy and she couldn't stop the tears that fell from her eyes. This was the one who had called to him in his dreams. This was the one he had fought to get to. She had to be his betrothed, his one true love. Who wouldn't desire her? She was perfection. Tanya turned away embarrassed, ashamed of her feelings.

"Child, be not ashamed. You are also welcomed here, if only temporarily."

Tanya realised that this young woman was talking to her and so she looked back.

"Who are you?"

"I am known as Rhiannon. And in answer to your unanswered question: Mathúin is not my betrothed. He is in fact, my son."

"How did you?" blurted Tanya, but then it registered what Rhiannon had just said. "Your—your son? But but he's older than you! And you're so young and … and beautiful!"

She smiled. "In your world, I would be over one hundred years of age. Time here flows … differently. That is why your visit here must be kept short."

Tanya looked at Matthew. He too was surprised at this news and took a step back.

"But we've only just arrived." He moved over to Tanya and put his arm round her. "Why would you want to send us back?"

Rhiannon's smile faltered, her face became sad. It was if a cloud had passed over the sun.

"Mathúin, you cannot go back. It is Tanya who must return."

Tanya felt as if she had been punched.

"What!" cried Matthew. "But I love her! We've only now found each other."

"Please, Mathúin, understand she doesn't belong here. She cannot stay."

"And I cannot return?"

"No, for if you do, you will surely die."

Matthew looked at Rhiannon in disbelief. "How?"

"When one of our kind ventures into their world," she glanced at Tanya in sympathy, "their bodies become poisoned with the toxins that exist there. We are creatures of magic and cannot survive in a world of science. Most only survive for a few years."

"But I managed to survive for thirteen years, and I feel fine." Matthew demanded.

Rhiannon sighed, she then looked to the others that stood around them and nodded slightly. As one, they all bowed and then walked back down the hillside towards the village. She turned back to Matthew and Tanya.

"Please sit."

Tanya looked at Matthew; he squeezed her hand and sat down. She moved next to him, resting her hand on his lap.

Rhiannon spent a moment watching them before sitting down.

"How much do you remember, Mathúin?"

"Not much, only that I needed to get here and that the Guardian is very dangerous." He then gazed off into the distance trying to remember. "And that, this place … is it called Alykeá?"

Rhiannon smiled and nodded. "Yes, it is. The need to get here and the knowledge of the Guardian are naturally the first things you will remember as they are aligned with your survival. Do you remember your father?"

"Rhiannon, Mother, I don't even remember you. What makes you think I'd remember my father any better?"

She closed her eyes and a small tear broke free to run down her perfect cheek. "Because you went back to find him."

"I—I did?"

"Your father was human, like Tanya." Opening her eyes, she looked at Tanya with such sadness Tanya had to avert her gaze. "We used to send groups to cross over and help repair nature in the new world for brief periods, in secrecy. It was during one of those times I met him accidentally. Love was instant, and I remember arguing with my parents about my feelings."

She chuckled "The irony is not lost on me. Anyway, I defied them and ran away to spend time with him in his world. But after a while I became sick, and I had to return to Alykeá. He was denied access to come back. We never saw each other again. But I then found myself with you, and I knew it was meant to be.

"I swore to never forget him and so, as you grew up I would tell you stories. I made sure that even though he couldn't be here, he still became very much an important part of your life. So much so, that when you came of age, you decreed that upon your first visit to the new world, you would go in search of him. I tried to talk you out of it, but you insisted. If I'm truthful to myself, part of me wanted you to succeed."

She stopped for a moment, as if to gather her thoughts. Neither Matthew or Tanya spoke, this was Rhiannon's story and they didn't want to disturb her.

"Such pain and tragedy happened on that cursed day. We no longer send anyone over now, it's too dangerous. We lost too many," she whispered.

Curious, Tanya spoke out, "Why, what happened?"

Rhiannon looked up, eyes misted with remembered pain. "The group entered the portal and for a long time we heard nothing. At first we assumed the work was taking longer than normal, it sometimes happens. But as time went on and still no message came, we began to worry. Finally, one of them managed to make it back through the portal, but only briefly, he died not long after.

"The Guardians had been waiting for us, something that had never happened before. Half the group was killed instantly, whilst the others had somehow managed to escape. These survivors tried to hide, but due to the chaos that surrounded them, they were soon separated. Too afraid to return to the portal, many of them died from the toxins. No one knew what happened to you, my son.

"I knew that you were half human and so I was confident you would survive longer than most. Most nights I prayed you had found your father and that he would protect you and that in time, return you to us. But as the months drew on, I started to fear I had lost you too.

"Then one night, you visited me through our dreams, and although I was overjoyed at seeing you, I realised you had no memory of me, nor of your people. Already I could see the sickness affecting you and feared time was against us. We had to get you to return to us as soon as possible, so we guided you through your dreams. It was hard and not without risk, but it worked and now you are here, safe," finished Rhiannon. The recounting had affected her badly as she appeared tired and drained.

Tanya looked at Matthew, or should she now call him Mathúin, she thought. He looks troubled. He's remembering. She couldn't even imagine the pain he must be going through, but there were still a few questions she didn't understand.

"Rhiannon, what are the Guardians? Wouldn't I be in danger from them too, when I return?"

"No child, they are from your world, so won't harm you. Your ancestors who feared and saw us as devils created them. In their eyes we didn't belong there and so they used these creatures to guard our portals. In time we learned to work around them, we knew what awoke them and so through our magic, we kept them at peace."

"But in the dreams," asked Tanya, "why have the storms?"

"The storms were not of our design; this is part of the magic of the Guardians. Once I realised Mathúin had forgotten his past, I realised he'd have no protection against them. We decided to … I believe your term for it is 'train' him? It was painful watching him go through it, but as you can now see, it was necessary."

She leaned over and placed a slender hand on Tanya's knee. "And now, I fear we must return you home. Alykeá is starting to affect you."

Mathúin quickly looked up from his musings and gasped when he looked at her. "Tanya?"

"What? I feel fine," she insisted.

He shook his head. "No, you're not. You're aging. Mother?"

"I'm sorry, my son, but there's nothing we can do."

"But we love each other!" he beseeched.

"Mathúin, I too had to make this decision. I know the pain you feel. Please don't let her die for your own selfish reasons."

"But they aren't selfish," interrupted Tanya. "I too love your son, can he not come back for a while? I don't want to lose him."

"There is nothing that can be done. You must let each other go."

Tears flowed freely down her cheeks as Rhiannon cupped Tanya's tear streaked face. "I'm so sorry, Tanya, but this love cannot be. We must send you back now, before it's too late."

"Matthew?" she cried.

"Tanya … I … I don't know what to do."

Instead, he reached out and held her close. His heart was close to breaking point, he could feel it tearing. He had just found his true home and yet at the same time, he had to let go of the one thing he loved the most. He couldn't deny that she was dying; she was aging right in front of him, and he now knew with certainty that he couldn't return either.

He pulled away and looked at her. "Sweetheart, you mu—" he choked on his tears, "you must go back, and I must stay here."

She started to shake her head, but he ignored her. "I will find a way to be with you. We've just found the existence of real magic and of other worlds. Anything is possible now." He kissed her. "We will be together again, I promise you! Don't lose hope, Tanya."

He hugged her tightly one last time, then with a tear stricken face looked to Rhiannon and nodded his agreement. Rhiannon slowly reached out and gently took Tanya by the shoulders, pulling her away.

A sob broke free, "No!"

"I'm so sorry, Tanya," she whispered.

Tanya stole one last look as she was herded to the portal and cried out, "I love you, Matthew!"

He could only smile, his pain was too much.

With an intense tearing sound, the world tore open again. A few seconds later, Tanya was surrounded by trees. The sun was out. She was home. She turned as the opening closed and saw Matthew whisper, "I love you."

THE PROPOSAL

The Proposal

Water sparkled like liquid silver in the moonlight. As the couple walked down the pathway, their laughter rang out amongst the rocks and trees. As they neared the lakeside, the boy placed a restraining hand on the girl's shoulder. "Hey, wait here a moment."

She turned and, going on tiptoes, placed a quick kiss on his lips. "Why?"

"Because I want this to be special, don't worry, I won't be long." As he walked off, he glanced back at her and smiled. "And no peeking!"

"Spoilsport!" she pouted.

Laughing, the boy ran off down the narrow pathway to the edge of the water and then along the shoreline until he came to an old tree stump where he had previously hidden a small package. Quickly he unfolded it into a blanket, laid it out, and took the selection of candles that had been placed in the centre. He then proceeded to position them strategically around the small site, before patting down his pockets looking for the lighter. He eventually found it in his back trouser pocket.

After lighting all the candles, the boy made a quick final check before running back to the girl. Everything's in order, he thought to himself, nothing can go wrong now. Hell, even the moon is in full glory with not a cloud in the sky!

Moments later, he found her sitting on a rock by a tree watching the stars. Her back was to him, so he quietly crept up behind. When he got as close as he dared, he stopped, slowly leaned in, and gently pushed his face into her mass of wavy dark hair, inhaling deeply her heavenly scent of vanilla. Immediately she jumped up and cried out in surprise. The boy stepped back laughing and she spun round to face him.

"Jees, Rob, you scared me!"

"I'm sorry, Carla, I couldn't resist. You smell too good!"

Pushing back her hair from her face, Carla smiled. "Flattery's not going to let you get out of this one. Scare me again and I'll have to punish you!"

"Wow, with an offer like th—ow!" Carla suddenly lunged out a playful punch and caught Rob on his arm. Fending her off, he raised his hands in submission "Okay, okay, I promise. I promise I won't do it again." Then he added under his breath with a mischievous look, "… at least not tonight."

Carla cried out in mock exasperation and threw a final punch, but Rob was prepared this time and caught her wrist. Quickly he pulled her towards him, wrapping her arm round his back, his other hand grabbing her other wrist and wrapped it round her back, locking their bodies tight against each other.

Looking up in to Rob's eyes, Carla whispered, "I seem to be trapped here."

"Uh huh. You noticed. And not doing a very good job of escaping either."

"No."

He leaned in and kissed her, slowly at first, but when she returned it, his passion mounted. He released her wrists and hugged her close, his right hand moving up her spine, cupping the base of her neck, fingers caressing her hair. Carla pulled herself up into his embrace by gripping the back of his shoulders, losing herself in the moment.

It lasted for a few moments and when they parted, it was with great reluctance. Carla gently clasped Rob's bottom lip between her teeth not wishing him to break away completely. He kissed her again, a teaser for later, and she released him.

"So … aren't you curious about my surprise?" Rob asked

"Can it beat this?"

"Yeah, but not by much."

"Then you'd better lead the way," she said. "I want to get back to where we left off."

Rob pulled away and held out his hand. Smiling, she took it and he led her down the pathway to the water's edge.

* * *

As the trees parted, Carla stopped, stunned by the beauty of the setting Rob had chosen. She was looking at a vision. Silhouetted trees flanked a small lake of black silver. Across from her, a tall, slim waterfall cascaded from a sheer cliff face. All around, a fine mist drifted out to create a gossamer effect. The moon's luminescent light was so bright it lit everything with an ethereal white shimmer, and, above, stars shone out as if they were diamonds cut from the fabric of fantasy. Carla felt as if she had just entered a dream.

"Oh my, it's … it's so beautiful," she whispered, her hand pressed tight against her heart. She turned and looked up at Rob's smiling face. "How?" But words failed her, and instead she wrapped her arms around him and kissed him hard.

"I take it you like it?" laughed Rob.

"Like it? I love it!"

They held each other for a moment before Rob released her and said, "Care for a seat?"

Carla looked back, her eyes drinking everything in, when she noticed the small blanket by the shoreline surrounded in candlelight and the mist creating small halos around each flame.

"Oh Rob, I don't know what to say."

"You don't need to, your eyes tell me everything."

"But, why?"

He gestured to the blanket, his face growing serious. "Carla, there's something I wish to ask you. But I have to tell you something else first."

Carla allowed herself to be led to the blanket and sat down. For a moment, Rob paced nervously before sitting down opposite her. He reached out, took her by the hand, and seemingly examined it as he gently stroked her skin with his thumb.

"Rob, are you okay?"

He sighed and looked up. "Carla, how long have we been together?"

"What?"

"How long?"

"A … about six months. Why?"

"And in all that time, have you ever been unhappy?"

She smiled. "I've never been happier in all my life. Rob, I love you!"

He smiled back. "And I love you too."

"So what's …?"

He raised his hand and stopped her question. She could see he was struggling with something. Part of her wanted to know what it was, she hated to see him in pain, but at the same time she was scared of what he was going to say.

"What if you learned something about me. Something that may change how you feel?"

"Why? Are you gay? Married? Oh God, you've got a kid?" she blurted.

"Ha!" His smile was genuine and warm. "No, I'd never do that to you. No, this is something quite different."

Raising his hand to her lips, she slowly kissed his palm. He closed his eyes and allowed himself to feel the softness of her lips and the warmth of her breath.

"If it's none of those, you've got nothing to worry about. Whatever it is, we'll face it together. My love for you is strong enough," she breathed.

He opened his eyes, smiled and leaned in. Cupping her face with his other hand he gently kissed her lips. "God, I love you so much."

But before she could return it, he pulled away. She could see he had finally decided on something by the way he looked at her. She guessed that it was good since he was still smiling.

"Come on," he said as he suddenly stood up.

"What?"

"Get up. I'm useless with words, so I'll just have to show you."

"Ok, but where are we going?" She didn't want to leave this haven, they'd only just arrived.

"Not far." His smile was becoming infectious. She found herself smiling in spite of her concerns.

He held out his hand. She took it and he pulled her up with surprising ease. Not letting go of her hand, Rob looked deeply into Carla's eyes and said, "Do you trust me?"

"Of course."

"Then I want you to put your arms around my neck."

Curious, she did as he asked, and he pulled her tight against him.

"Now, close your eyes," he whispered into her ear, his breath warm, "and follow my movements."

"Are we going to dance?" she smiled.

"You could say that. Are your eyes closed?"

"Yes," she whispered.

"Now, don't let go." And with that she felt Rob tense slightly as he bent his knees and jumped.

Something was wrong. They should have landed.

Rob moved his lips close to her ear and whispered, "Open your eyes."

She did. They hadn't landed, because they were still in the air—ten feet in the air and slowly rising. She couldn't help herself as she tightened her arms round Rob's neck.

"What the—" but she couldn't talk. She couldn't believe what she was seeing.

"Rob?" she squeaked.

They were flying.

"Don't worry, I have you," he said.

She turned and saw him smile at her before looking out over her shoulder.

Correction … he was flying! Rob could fly! Carla's senses screamed out this wasn't possible. This defied all the laws of physics. How could he … fly? She looked all around, looking for a rope or something … anything to explain this … this …

"My God, we're flying!" she yelped. She couldn't see anything attached, nor could she feel a harness on Rob. Regardless of what her rational mind insisted, she had, for the time being, to accept that her Rob could defy reality … that her Rob could fly.

Rob looked back at her, he could tell she was freaked out by what was happening, but he also knew she was strong and that their love was powerful enough to ride out the initial shock, she'd just proven that. Besides, who doesn't dream of flying at some point in their life?

When she finally looked back at him, he saw within her eyes a dawning of realization, the initial look of pure terror was being replaced with a look of wonder. She smiled that amazing smile she only shared with him and laughed aloud. He laughed back, and together they looked out across the lake. Gracefully, they flew towards the waterfall. Carla's long hair dancing about in the breeze, the spray caressing their skin, the sound of water thundering in their ears.

As they neared, he allowed Carla to reach out with one hand and thrust it into the falling water, letting her feel the weight pummel against her. She giggled at his cry, as she cupped her wet hand against his cheek. In retaliation he shot the two of them up twenty feet, causing Carla to squeal out in surprise and wrap her arms tightly around his neck. He slowed to a stop, hovering in the air.

Far below their dangling feet, the lake surface danced in the moonlight; the waterfall, just out of reach, rumbled past them. Time slowed and they found themselves gazing into each other's eyes, Carla calmly leaned forward and kissed Rob tenderly. He responded in kind, and together they lost themselves to the magic of the moment.

Blissfully unaware, they gradually started to rise again, slowly rotating high up into the night sky, leaving the waterfall and the lake far, far below them. A few minutes passed and Rob and Carla reluctantly pulled away, breathless.

Kissing her forehead briefly, he whispered, "Look around."

"Oh my!"

The view below, literally took Carla's breath away. She could see for miles in every direction, she estimated they must be at least two hundred feet up in the air. It was like looking down on a model of fields and woodland, the moonlight covered everything in a silver sheen. She could make out the trees, the old road Rob had driven them down earlier, she could even see his car parked, hidden among the bushes. On the horizon, lit up by a thousand orange stars, was the city.

Below, the lake looked like a mirror, reflecting the stars and moon in its crystal waters, the waterfall, just a gentle murmur. The air was so clear up here, the moon so swollen, and, for the first time in a long time, she knew what it felt to be totally free, to have no constraints. She loved Rob with all of her heart, but what he was giving her now was more than mere words could express. Tears started to appear in her eyes. She quickly buried her face in his neck, hoping he wouldn't see.

Realizing that Carla may need some time to take in all that had happened, Rob slowly descended towards the edge of the waterfall.

Carla felt the hardness of the ground touch her feet, but she couldn't let go of Rob, she didn't want to let go of that magical moment they had shared. It wasn't until Rob had reached back and taken hold of her hands, that she allowed him pull away. Although he noticed her tear stained face, he didn't make an issue of it.

"I suppose you've got a few questions?" he asked.

"A, a few? Rob, you can fly!"

She looked around. Wiping her face, she realized Rob had landed them atop the waterfall. Below, she could make out the blanket and candles. It seemed like hours had passed since they were down there. Everything had changed: she was now living in a world where people can fly! "How is this even possible?" she heard herself whisper.

"I … I don't know. I've always been able to since I was a kid," he answered. "I've always been careful though, making sure no one saw me. Nighttime is usually the only time I get to be totally free."

He walked over to the very edge of the cliff, the waterfall roaring to his right, and looked out over the horizon. "I couldn't let anyone know. I don't know what they'd do to me if they ever found out? I don't want to be seen as some kind of … some kind of freak!"

Carla stood still, not wanting to get too close to the edge. "Rob, you're not a freak. My God, you're an angel, you can fly! Don't you realize how beautiful this is? What you can do … it's a miracle!"

He turned to face her and smiled. "You won't tell anyone will you?"

"God, I'd never. Rob, what you've shown me—no, what you've given me is so special, so magical. I … I can't even explain what you mean to me. What this means to me. Ha!" she laughed. "My boyfriend can fly!"

Rob couldn't help but laugh with her, even if it did sound a bit forced. After a moment, Carla looked up at Rob, her head turned slightly to the side. Here it comes, thought Rob. He knew what her next question was going to be, even before she asked it. It was the one he had been waiting for.

"Rob?" She edged closer to him. "If you've been keeping this a secret for all this time, why tell me?"

Bang! There it was! He took a deep breath. All his plans for this night had lead to this moment. He suddenly found his mouth dry.

"Carla, since the moment we laid eyes on each other, my heart has been yours. I feel we are connected in ways I can't even explain. I love you so totally, so completely, that I want to be with you always, together forever. Heh, that sounds so corny, but it's true."

Carla reached out and took Rob's hand in hers, she sensed what was coming and wanted to help Rob, to give him some of her strength, to let him know it was okay.

Looking down he continued, "But in order to do that, I need to be totally honest with you. I have to show you the real me, otherwise anything we have would be a sham, a lie."

Rob looked up at Carla. "I could never do that to you. By sharing this secret with you, I have exposed myself to you, I have bared my soul. But I believe in us. I believe in our love. I can see it in your eyes each and every day I look at you."

Taking a deep breath, he stepped back and slowly lowered himself down onto one knee. "Carla … will you marry me?"

Out of nowhere, Rob produced a simple ring with a single diamond set into it, the facets capturing the moonlight turned it into a star. She didn't care he could fly, and she'd keep his secret to the grave. She loved him more than anything. This night just confirmed that. A single tear broke free and she fell to her knees.

"Yes!" she whispered.

ORIGINS

Origins

The doe fell without a sound, a single slim shaft protruding from her left flank, the heart pierced.

Culowyn was pleased as he ran over to the corpse. Here was enough meat to feed them all for the next couple of days. Although Ardovan had provisioned them well to last out the winter, Culowyn still enjoyed the hunt. Besides, he enjoyed proving to his older brother, Aiden, he was the better archer.

Crouching down beside the animal, he carefully pulled out the arrow, making sure not to snap it. Once free, he grabbed an old bowstring from his belt pouch and tied the doe's four legs together. When he was sure they were secure, Culowyn lowered his head and swung the creature onto his back. He grunted with the weight, but after a few adjustments he managed to get the balance right. He then picked up his bow and started to make his way back to the cabin, whistling quietly to himself.

It was a beautiful winter's morning. Everywhere the ground was blanketed in virgin white. Naked trees stood scattered about with branches that were overburdened with thick coats of snow. Above, the sun dazzled in all her brilliance for there was not a cloud in the azure sky.

Culowyn felt good and breathed in deeply the crisp frosty air. He loved these kind of mornings, although that hadn't always been the case. Five years past, when Ardovan had first hid him and his brother out here in the mountains, he had been a young and impetuous brat, brought up soft and weak from within the confines of their father's castle, Ghan Keep. But that had all changed when their father, Lord Govan, had been brutally murdered.

A sudden flood of memories washed over him, causing Culowyn to pause and shiver in the morning breeze. Last night had been the anniversary of their exile, and the bottle had been passed freely between the three of them as they spoke of remembered times. Ardovan finally confessed to the truth of what happened to their father and captain.

* * *

"... heh ... Da never did get 'round to apologising to Lady Scarlotta in the end," giggled Aiden before taking another deep draft.

"Come on, you can't be serious!" Culowyn exclaimed. "Even after all that Telsin did for him?"

"Uh huh. Though Telsin did try to get his revenge on Da, but Da was too clever. They decided in the end to just settle the matter like lords and drank their way through a barrel of delerian red."

"Ha! That's so like Da! Though I imagine Ma wasn't too pleased in the morning."

"You can say that again! Da said that at the time he'd have preferred to have faced the entire Slaver Wars again!"

Both boys fell about laughing.

Smiling his crooked smile, Ardovan reached out and quickly grabbed the bottle from Aiden's limp grasp. Taking a mighty swig from it, he held the bottle high and barked, "A canny man was Lord Govan and a fearsome captain upon the battlefield!"

"Aye, to Da!" cried the boys in unison, each holding forth an imaginary bottle in mimicry of Ardovan.

They smiled at each other as silence settled over them like a warm winter's blanket and their thoughts turned inwards. In the background, the fire crackled gently, filling the room with warmth and soft dancing shadows.

After a while, Culowyn looked over at the creased and weathered face of their guardian and asked, "Ardovan, what happened that night?" He didn't need to say which night.

Ardovan looked over. A shadow passed over the room. Aiden's ears perked up at the question, and he looked expectantly at the two of them.

After a beat, Ardovan muttered, "Lord Govan was murdered and that's all you need to know." He looked back into the flames, taking a swift pull from the bottle. "And, you're still too young."

"Uh uh, not this time Ardovan. You told us that you'd tell us the truth only when the both of us had come of age. Well, Aiden was sixteen last year. and this year's my turn. So, please Ardovan. Tell us. We deserve to know!" pleaded Culowyn.

Ardovan turned back to look at the two boys and sighed heavily, this wasn't going to be easy for him. He had tried to lose the memories of that cursed night, but when he looked upon Lord Govan's beloved sons, he saw their father's famed determination echo in their steel grey eyes. He lowered the bottle poised to his lips.

They were right, of course. They were no longer the two scared boys he'd rescued five years past, but young men about to come into their prime. Both had their father's build and good looks, his strong chin, and penetrating stare, but their pinched noses were stolen from their mother. The only difference between them was that Aiden had inherited his father's dark brown hair, while Culowyn's was golden, just like Lady Govan.

He sighed again and nodded. "Aye, you're right, Culowyn. You both deserve to know the truth. But it ain't gonna be easy." Ardovan took another sip and ushered the boys closer, they complied readily.

"You've both heard tales of 'The Griffin,' Lord Govan's company and one I'm proud to say I served?"

Aiden nodded. "Of course! Who hasn't? Why, they're famous. You're famous. I mean you were part of the legend that won us the Slaver War."

Ardovan couldn't help but smile at the enthusiasm that sparkled in their eyes.

"Aye. But fame is such a fickle thing. It's one that can and will betray you if not treated with respect.

"Unfortunately your father was too modest, he always felt uncomfortable whenever his deeds were mentioned. This alienated those who coveted his glory and soon they forgot his accomplishments and instead looked upon him with eyes of jealousy."

"But why?" asked Culowyn. "Da had saved them."

"Why? He had a beautiful wife, a home that was the pride of the county, the ear of the King, and most importantly, the love of the people." Ardovan paused and took another drink before passing the bottle to Culowyn. "If only he hadn't cared so much for them.

"The people came to him for advice, for aid, and soon his word became law in the county. Not that your father approved of it, of course, he desperately tried to explain there were others who they should go to, but they all trusted him, and thus fame started to play her cruel trick. Through his actions in the war and all the legends that followed, he had proven himself to be a man of honour, a man who stood by his word, a man who defended those less fortunate. And before he knew it, your father had been ensnared into the treacherous web of politics.

"Now you would think the battlefield would be a dangerous place to be in," Ardovan shook his head. "But no, at least there you could face your enemy, look him in the eyes before striking him down." His gaze wavered as he glanced at the flames.

"In the halls of Parliament, you never knew who your enemy was: that was a very hard lesson for your father to learn. He always believed in honesty and the law. Unfortunately, a few decided to use that virtue to their own advantage."

"He was betrayed?" asked Aiden.

"Aye, Aiden, by the very ones Lord Govan was defending. You see, war is a very costly venture in both lives and the coffers; it was because of this that the Vistari soon found themselves in dire trouble and urgently needed support from the Parliament. Monetary support, if you know what I mean. So they befriended the only man who had that power: Lord Govan."

"The Vistari?" queried Aiden. "I think I remember Da mentioning them before."

"I expect you would have. They are part of the Merchants Guild and once a respected group, that is until Marco Spirensi took control. He and five other counselors of the Vistari decided to use the support of Lord Govan to obtain the loans they needed to clear their debts.

"But when Marco saw the name of Lord Govan had more influence than his own, jealousy seeped into the cracks, and he began to plan a way to steal that fame. He soon realised no one checked the accounts of Lord Govan. I mean why should they? He was their war hero! So he created false invoices to fictitious creditors to leech more money for his own coffers. In the beginning, he had started off with small amounts, but these then quickly grew in size as his own greed increased."

Ardovan paused and stoked the fire, sending thousands of sparks to drift up the chimney. Culowyn and Aiden sat waiting.

"Lord Govan soon found out and confronted Marco. He was furious and demanded Marco repay all that he had stolen, but Marco had already put in play his plan. You don't need to know the details suffice to say that hidden within the false invoices, Marco had purposely left clues that questioned Lord Govan's loyalties.

"It all came to a head one cursed day when Marco realised that after the confrontation with Lord Govan, his pretense could not be sustained for much longer and so he presented the Parliament with his 'proof.' This damning evidence stated that the reason Lord Govan had been so successful in the Slaver Wars, was because he himself was a Slaver. Through cunning and deceit, Marco claimed the reason for Lord Govan numerous victories against the enemy was because of inside sources. Spies, if you like, who helped him lay down plans to wipe out all the Lords who would have opposed his claim and then, the minute he found all competition eliminated, snatched the title of Slaver Lord for himself!"

Culowyn quickly leapt up, outraged. "But that's impossible and a downright lie!"

"He was the most honorable man alive!" exclaimed Aiden. "He risked his life time and again for those ungrateful—"

"Will you both calm down!" barked Ardovan. "I'm telling it like it is, and if you don't like it, well, then, I suppose the two of you had best go to bed as you're proving yourself to be too young to hear the truth!"

The two boys twitched as they looked at Ardovan's stern glare and then at each other. Both wanted to shout out their anger, but at the same time wanted to hear the rest of the story. Reason quickly prevailed and soon both sat down, indicating to Ardovan to continue.

Ardovan grunted and leaned into the circle. "We knew the truth," he rasped, jabbing his thumb into his chest. "We knew that Lord Govan was one of the most loyal men we've ever had the pleasure to serve under. We fought by his side. We listened to his counsel. We trusted him and would have followed him to the gates of Helviti itself!"

Ardovan looked down. "But from what I've heard, Marco's proof was pretty convincing. I had no idea Marco would sink so low for a pretty coin. Fortunately, there were still a couple of members in Parliament who saw the lies for what they were and immediately sent out an envoy to Ghan Keep to forewarn Lord Govan of the treachery of the Vistari.

"Alas the scandal split the people down the middle, so those who trusted Lord Govan flocked to Ghan Keep to stand by their Lord. You may have noticed the increase in traffic during those final days?" The two boys both nodded their agreement.

"Lord Govan wanted to protect you two from these lies, he was hoping that once the rest of Parliament realised the truth, the order would be restored and Marco would be punished for betraying the people. Therefore, he kept you busy with chores and constant training, deftly moving you about like pawns in a chess game.

"Some believe that the first attack was upon Lady Govan, when she contracted the sickness that killed her." Ardovan looked down and whispered, "May Hulda protect her."

Culowyn looked across at Aiden and saw his brother desperately trying to blink away his tears. Their mother's death had been a long and painful one. When she had finally passed away, she was no longer the beautiful woman they'd remembered, but a withered and skeletal shell.

"But there was no proof and although her death devastated Lord Govan, he never gave up his fight against the lies of Marco.

"But then it happened." Ardovan sighed and sat back, he ran his hands through his cropped hair and took a moment. The two boys looked at each other, they hadn't seen Ardovan look this hesitant before, and it was disheartening to see.

Swallowing, Culowyn reached over and gently touched Ardovan on the hand. "Ardovan, you don't have to continue if you don't want to, we, we have our memories."

Ardovan shook his head, and smiled, he raised his hand and ruffled Culowyn's hair. "No lad, you deserve to know the truth, both of you. You are your father's sons alright, and there isn't a day that I don't feel pride in seeing you grow. Your father would have been proud of the both of you."

He took a steadying breath. "As you know, Ghan Keep was attacked. It was a cowardly act, for mercenaries entered during the night and assassinated the guards at the gates. They then forced them open, allowing the Vistaris' hired army to enter unopposed. They rode in and ran down anyone who so much as raised a fist against them.

"The minute the alarm was raised, Lord Govan called forth The Griffin, and we met them in the courtyard. The fighting was fierce and too many good men lost their lives there for the area was too confined, we couldn't move. But then the villagers and townsmen who had come to Lord Govan to lend him their support, saw the bloodshed and futility in the battle and instead of running, they—" Ardovan's voice broke, and he quickly grabbed the bottle and drank deeply.

Wiping his mouth dry with the back of his bracers, he looked off into the distance as if he was hearing the screams of that night again echo within his mind. "They grabbed any kind of weapon they could find and ran to our aid. These simple folk, farmers, bakers, they all loved and adored your father. He was more than a lord to them. He was their hero, he was their hope, and they fought for him, without orders, without prompt. They fought purely out of love. I'd never seen the like before.

"It was at this point that Lord Govan called me to his side. He told me to wake the two of you and take you away from Ghan Keep, to take the secret way and hide you in the wilderness. It was then I realised what he had planned. I refused to go, saying I wanted to stay and fight by his side.

"But when he turned to look at me, tears were in his eyes and he said simply 'Look after my boys, Ardovan, teach them everything you know. Now go, my friend, and goodbye,' and he went back out to fight along side the townsmen.

"As I entered the Great Hall, I looked back and watched your father's final stand.

"Lord Govan had called a stop to the fighting. He pleaded that no more innocent lives were to be lost on his account. He surrendered his sword and laid it upon the ground.

"Marco Spirensi then entered Ghan Keep and walking forward, announced in a loud voice, for all to hear, the charges that were to be brought forward.

"The Parliament had found Lord Govan guilty of treason to the crown and was therefore sentenced to death, but because of his distinguished record, he would be executed as a soldier.

"Marco walked right up to Lord Govan and even though your father was surrounded by the enemy and covered in blood, I never saw him look more noble. There was a brief exchange of words, but then Marco suddenly spat into your father's face. There was an outcry, but Lord Govan raised his hand and called for order. He then slowly wiped the spittle from his face and looked at Marco.

"Marco called for the guard to manacle the traitor and turned away. But then once they had cuffed him, Marco cried out 'This piece of filth doesn't deserve a soldiers death!' and he spun on his heel, there was a flash of steel, a gout of blood and … and …" Ardovan covered his face with his hands, his eyes were crimson and he took a few steadying breaths. After a moment, he slowly rose his head and looked straight in to the eyes of Aiden and Culowyn. "Lord Govan collapsed to the ground, his throat severed by a blunt and notched knife. He had been murdered in cold blood!"

The two boys sat there in silence, tears running freely down their cheeks. They knew their father had died at the Keep, but they had always assumed he had been killed in battle, defending the weak, not slaughtered like cattle, manacled and defenseless.

"Anyway, I, er, eh hem, I quickly realised Marco would want your deaths too. So I ran and woke you both, stealing you away via the secret way as agreed.

Marco was furious when he found out you had escaped unharmed and immediately placed a bounty on your heads. To this day that bounty still stands and we have been in hiding ever since."

Aiden tried to speak, but his throat constricted. He only managed a horse whisper. "Did, did anyone try and avenge Father's murder?"

Ardovan looked at the fire, watching the flames dance to soundless music. "Aiden, you must understand. These were simple folk; they were scared. Everything they knew had been taken from them. Lord Govan was no longer there to defend them, The Griffin were no more, they had been ordered to disband immediately. Any mention of Lord Govan's name meant certain death. So, no, his murder has never been avenged."

The fire crackled in the silence as the three lowered their heads. A pall had fallen upon the room as the bottle was passed quietly around.

* * *

The howl of a wolf brought Culowyn back to the present, no doubt the animal was starved and could smell the blood of the doe; he sighed and forced the memories back as he marched his way forward. Now would not be a good time to be caught unaware.

About a half an hour later, Culowyn found himself looking down upon an old log cabin at the bottom of a valley. Smoke trailed lazily out of the chimney and he smiled, anticipating the look of envy on Aiden's face. Carefully, he made his way down the slope, using the trees as support, the carcass was getting heavier, and he found his legs were starting to turn to jelly.

Just to the side of the cabin was a small shelter. It was here that Culowyn deposited the doe. Pulling out his hunting knife, he began to quickly work on it, first slicing the carcass to aid bleeding, and then hanging it. By the time he was finished, Culowyn was tired and in need of a wash.

"Aiden!" he shouted. "Give us a hand here!" but there was no answer. Swearing to himself, Culowyn grabbed his hunting knife and made his way to the cabin. Lazy bastard, no doubt sleeping off last night's drink, thought Culowyn as he pushed his way through the front door. "Hey Aiden, get your lazy arse up! I need a hand carrying my kill!"

The room was empty. If it wasn't for the inviting warmth from the fire and scattered clothing, Culowyn would have thought that there was no one home. Grumbling to himself, he made his way over to the kitchen table and dumped the knife.

"Aiden!"

Still no reply.

Culowyn walked over to the basin and filled it with water from the jug. Briskly he scrubbed the congealing blood from his hands and dried them off on an old piece of cloth.

Sighing in resignation, he walked back into the living room and started picking up the various bits of clothing, allowing himself violent thoughts on what he'd like to do to his brother once he caught up with him.

His world stopped when Culowyn noticed fresh blood pooled near the hearth. Slowly he looked around the room again. This time he noticed all the obvious signs scattered about that he'd initially missed. He could see other patches of blood, not enough to cause concern, but he then saw that both Aiden's and Ardovan's swords were missing. Clothes weren't the only items in disarray either; the furniture had been tussled too. It soon became obvious that either a fight or scuffle had recently broken out.

Running to the door, he quickly he grabbed his own sword, belted it on, then ran out to the small hut and took up his bow and quiver. Strapping the quiver to his back, Culowyn returned to the porch and quickly scanned the ground; a clear set of tracks in the snow lead off down the valley.

Fortunately, the snow was still fresh from the early morning fall and so Culowyn was able to run alongside the trail. His fear rose when he noticed that the blood had stained the snow at regular intervals. Whoever it was, had been badly wounded. He prayed that it wasn't Aiden or Ardovan.

He ran for about five minutes before he could make out the sounds of fighting echoing off in the distance. Sprinting forward, Culowyn soon crested a small hill. About a quarter of a mile away out in the open, Ardovan stood defending himself against three assailants, Aiden was kneeling on the ground behind Ardovan clutching his shoulder, two dead bodies flanked them.

Every part of Culowyn wanted to run to his brother's aid, but instinct held him back. He moved quickly to the tree line to his left and, notching an arrow, quietly moved through the trees. Moments later he thanked the Gods for his foresight when he noticed movement within the brush overlooking the battle scene. An archer had positioned himself so that he could survey the area, if Culowyn had rushed in, the archer would have had an easy death shot. They had obviously anticipated Culowyn arriving.

Ignoring a cold shiver that ran across his soul at this realization, Culowyn took aim and released his arrow. The aim was true and the archer collapsed with barely a grunt. Ignoring the corpse for the time being, Culowyn quickly looked out and realized he was too far away to aid Ardovan and Aiden with his bow and still remain hidden, he would have to expose himself, but at least he could take down one of them before resorting to the blade.

Notching another arrow, Culowyn quickly ran from the cover of the trees and down the gentle slope closing the distance. Ardovan was battling furiously and another assailant suddenly fell, his lifeblood splashing out from a vicious cut to the stomach. But Ardovan was tiring and the two remaining attackers flanking Ardovan could see this. Crying out in defiance, they both threw themselves recklessly against him as waves against a rock. But this rock was old and Ardovan stumbled.

"Ardovan!" cried Culowyn. The assailants were now too close for him to take aim.

Throwing his bow to the ground, Culowyn carelessly sprinted towards the fight, desperately trying to pull free his sword. Everything slowed down to a painful pace. One of the men managed to break through Ardovan's weakened defense and cut him deeply across the thigh. Ardovan grunted and staggered back, briefly exposing Aiden. Seeing the opening, the other fighter was quick to thrust his blade across Aiden's neck, slicing open his throat. Blood blossomed from the cut and Aiden gasped, stained hands desperately tried to stem the flow to no avail.

"No!" screamed Culowyn.

Time rushed back with a fury as Culowyn slammed into Aiden's killer, knocking them both to the ground with a grunt. Enraged beyond control, Culowyn forgot all about his training from Ardovan and literally tore into his stunned assailant like a wild animal. His sword lying forgotten in the snow beside him, Culowyn's fingers instead ripped open the man's leather jerkin allowing him to lunge in fast, biting deep into the scarred neck, ripping the flesh open.

The man screamed out in agony and desperately tried to push Culowyn away, but Culowyn was resolute. He clung on like a savage and kept tearing into the neck with both fingernails and teeth. Blood sprayed out as he bit his way through the arteries.

Only when he could no longer feel the warm blood splatter across his cheek, did Culowyn pull back, leaving the corpse to the crows.

Bloodlust and anger were still upon him. He turned to face the remaining fighter, but he found him splayed out across the snow, his head severed. Ardovan grunted and fell to his knees, the notched blade of a broadsword protruded from his back.

"Gods, Ardovan!" gasped Culowyn, and he quickly reached out and caught him as slumped sideways.

Ardovan coughed violently and blood exploded out from his lips. "I think ... they've ..." He stopped to catch his breath. "... they've found us."

"Don't you dare leave me, Ardovan!" cried Culowyn.

"'Fraid I can't help ... help you there ... boy ... I already hear ... Hulda calling."

Ardovan's breathing became labored as he found it more and more difficult to talk. He reached up and grabbed Culowyn by his collar, pulling him closer. Tear stricken, Culowyn leaned in putting his ear next to Ardovan's bloodied lips.

"Culo ... wyn ... you must ... you must not avenge me ... nor ... your brother ... You must stay hidden! ... It ... was ... your father's ... last ... last wish."

Ardovan's head drooped, he was barely breathing now.

"How can I? They've taken everything from me." He looked across at his brother who was still kneeling, his chin rested on his still chest and his arms hung uselessly by his side, his clothes and surrounding snow were drenched in cooling blood. "I have nothing left to keep me hidden. Nothing to protect!" Culowyn felt anger build up deep within him as tears streamed down his blood-soaked cheeks.

"We have done nothing to deserve this! Why should I hide and they live on with their open lies?"

Culowyn looked down at Ardovan, but Ardovan was no longer listening. Gently he lowered the man down who had, for the past five years, been his closest friend and mentor. Numb fingers gently closed the lids of Ardovan's glassy eyes and Culowyn allowed himself to feel his grief wash over him.

* * *

Later that day, standing over two shallow graves marked only by two swords stabbed into the frozen earth, Culowyn slowly picked up his backpack. He was wearing his leather jerkin and trousers, with Ardovan's shirt of chainmail over the top. A mixture of belts held his weapons around his slim waist, his father's longsword, a short stabbing sword, and a slim hunting knife. Two daggers were carefully hidden within his soft hunting boots and his bow with a quiver full of arrows was strapped to his back.

"Farewell, my brother. Greet Da and Ma for me, they shall not find you a disappointment … you fought bravely." Culowyn said to the first grave.

Then slowly he turned to the second and through gritted teeth he said, "Ardovan, it may have been my father's last wish, but I am now a man. I demand that justice be paid for the murder of my family and dearest friend!"

Drawing his hunting knife, he grasped the blade with his free hand and quickly pulled the blade free, cutting his palm. He allowed the blood to drip onto both of the graves, then closing his eyes, he lifted his face skyward and whispered, "May Hulda watch over both your souls."

He then looked down upon both graves and with cold eyes stated, "I shall honour your dying wish Ardovan. Culowyn shall disappear into the mists of time. From this day forth I shall be known only as Ardovan in honor of you, and they will learn to fear our name, for I will hunt them down, each and everyone one of those dogs! Our family will be avenged! This I swear!"

* * *

Marco slowly poured the dark bitter liquid that was a delicacy from the far southern states into a small fragile cup. Taking a sip, he grimaced and decided to sweeten it with a touch more honey. He had been up most of the night going over the accounts and had been told that this carrafea would help him keep his wits fresh. So far, it seemed to be working, but it couldn't help him with his current problem: trying to find a way to hide the latest of his illicit taxes. This year was proving to be very profitable, and he didn't want the Crown to reap his hard earned cash.

A sharp tap came from the oak door and without looking up Marco barked out, "I said I didn't want to be disturbed!"

"But my Lord, I have news regarding your ... problem," replied a confident voice.

Marco paused in his work and slowly looked up, his calculations all but forgotten, his face a mixture of emotions.

"Well enter then ... and be quick!"

The door opened and in stepped a short middle-aged balding man dressed in dark leather. Across his chest was a bandolier holding several throwing knives and at his hip rested a slim rapier. Upon seeing Marco, he bowed deeply.

"My Lord, our network has been successful in locating Ardovan."

"And you have him captured?" asked Marco expectantly.

"I fear not … at least not yet. But we are closing in on him even now as we speak."

"He's here? In Hawkpoint already?"

The man looked up and smiled. "Yes my Lord."

But Marco wasn't so confident, for the past three years each of his colleagues in the Vistari had been found brutally murdered by this man known only as Ardovan. His brazen nature had made their own personal guards a mockery in the eyes of the Crown.

Marco was now the last one left alive from the initial group and so had spent a considerable amount of money trying to find out what he could on this killer, but the only thing his enquiries could uncover was that of a Captain Ardovan who had once fought alongside Lord Govan in the outlawed unit, The Griffin. But he would have been old even then after they had managed to disband the renegades. He must be ancient now, much too old to accomplish what this young pretender was rumored to have done.

No, this was someone else, someone who should have died a long time ago. He had his suspicions, but it brought back too many unpleasant memories. If he was to be brutally honest with himself, it was a time of which even Marco felt ashamed, particularly of his actions that resulted in the cold hearted and savage murder of Lord Govan.

"Your orders my Lord?"

Marco found his musings broken by the request. He slowly looked up into the cold eyes of his agent. "Your orders are to find and kill this upstart. Gather your best men and take no chances. He must die tonight!"

"Yes, my Lord."

As the door closed, Marco tried to get back to his work but found his concentration was disturbed. The room was getting darker, the candles had burned low and looking out of the window Marco surmised it must be getting close to dawn. A sudden yawn took him by surprise and so he decided that maybe a few hours sleep should help clear his head better than the carrafea.

Closing his books, Marco slowly made his way through the door where he was greeted by two bodyguards who quickly stood to attention upon seeing him.

"At ease, men. It's late. I'm going to my quarters to catch some rest."

Obediently they fell into position behind Marco and followed him down the corridor.

* * *

The kindling had caught quickly and within moments the fireplace roared into life. Rubbing his hands over the naked flames, Marco quickly glanced around the room, his eyes lingered around the four-poster bed and the various wardrobes, each time taking note of the familiar shadows that flickered to life from the fire.

Reluctantly, he found his gaze being drawn to the curtains, which draped across the double doors leading out onto the balcony. A balcony that was at least eighty feet above the courtyard and was heavily guarded by the some of the best mercenaries money could buy.

His mouth felt dry. The news of Ardovan's presence within the city of Hawkpoint had obviously unnerved him more than he was willing to admit. He tried to shrug off his growing anxiety as he turned towards his bed. Suddenly he stopped still, his eyes quickly drawn back to the curtains. He wasn't sure, but for a moment, he could have sworn they had moved. Without taking his eyes from the embroidered material, he slowly reached down to the bejeweled stiletto dagger belted to his hip and quietly drew the blade free.

The room was quite large, but that evening, Marco felt that it was the entire length of Alykeá. As if walking on eggshells, he walked across the expanse, watchful for any movement. Halfway across he could feel his heart beating madly against his ribs like a caged wild animal desperate to get out. Cold sweat beaded across his forehead threatening to blind him with its pregnant droplets.

Painfully he made it across the room, but just as he reached out to grab the curtains, they suddenly moved again. Marco couldn't help but yelp out in shock.

Fearing Ardovan would suddenly leap out, Marco viciously stabbed the material. Unfortunately his thrust was clumsy and he fell forward abruptly onto the small balcony, tearing the curtain free from it's rail.

Marco quickly released the dagger and rolled over. Eyes squeezed shut he raised his arm high over his face hoping to thwart the blow from Ardovan's sword. After a few agonizing seconds of nothing, Marco dared to open his eyes a fraction and look up over his raised arm. No one was there. It was just him, the fading stars, and an over active imagination.

He quickly glanced around, but the balcony was empty. He turned onto his stomach and carefully looked through the gaps of the stone rail, peering over the ledge. Nothing, just a straight drop down to the courtyard. He could even make out a group of his guards playing dice next to the closed gates. Resting his head against the stone he closed his eyes and finally let out his breath; it was only then that he realised that he had been holding it in the entire time. He allowed himself a few moments to compose himself and then roughly got to his knees. It took a couple of minutes as the curtain had tangled with his legs.

Marco threw the torn material to the side as he walked back into his room and briskly got undressed and into his bed garments. He was furious at himself for allowing his imagination to get the better of him and if he was honest, quite a bit embarrassed. Pulling back the bed sheets, he quickly got in and tried to calm his nerves enough to fall asleep. The last thing that he noticed was the dying flames of his kindling.

* * *

The guard slumped noiselessly as Ardovan quickly clasped him to his breast and gently lowered the body to the ground. He withdrew his stiletto from the base of guard's skull and wiped it clean on the discarded cloak. Glancing over the body of the second dead guard, Ardovan took note of the last die roll and realised the guard he had just killed would have won the game.

Leaning down he whispered into the guard's ear, "Never let your guard down. Remember that as you stand before Helviti's Gates"

Ardovan withdrew and quickly looked around the courtyard. All of the guards that were posted with a view of the tower were now dispatched and those due to replace them had also been removed. It was just him and Marco now.

Ardovan rose from his crouch and slowly shed the disguise of a hired mercenary. He had made sure he had been recruited by one of Marco's lackeys a week ago when his carefully laid rumor had finally blossomed. A week to learn the motions of the estate, a week to plan.

He took a deep breath, as he calmed his apprehension. It had been four long years since Ardovan and Aiden had been brutally murdered and finally Ardovan nee Culowyn could feel the end of his quest for vengeance.

Sheathing the stiletto, Ardovan ran swiftly across the courtyard and leaped up the base of the tower to the first set of handholds he had noticed earlier during one of his patrols. Then with a speed born from experience, Ardovan scaled the eighty-foot tower like a spider, using nothing but skill and determination.

Within minutes, Ardovan grasped hold of the stone railings and effortlessly lifted himself onto them. Crouching like a gargoyle, he quickly surveyed the area and immediately noticed the torn curtain abandoned in a pile. A smile creased his lips as he imagined Marco's fear taking control. But that could also be a two-edged sword; it could mean that Marco may have taken steps to protect himself. Unlikely, but possible. Arrogance could only take you so far.

Silently Ardovan lowered himself onto the balcony and entered Marco's room through the open double doors. Heavy breathing could be heard coming from the bed but not much could be seen as the fire had died down to a few burning embers. Sticking to the shadows, he prowled the room, searching the corners and checking the door for additional guards.

There was no threat of discovery. The room appeared brighter since he first arrived and as Ardovan regarded the open doorway across the room, he noticed that the dawning sun was just surfacing.

Ardovan glided over to the four-poster bed and gazed down upon the sleeping form of his nemesis. Finally, he thought to himself, I get to avenge my father and family, you murdering bastard! Then reaching round to the small of his back, he unhooked a slip of silk rope. He scanned the bedposts and smiled when he found enough carvings to secure the rope to.

Stretching out, Ardovan tenderly took hold of one of Marco's wrists and slipped the rope around it, being careful not to disturbed the sleeping form. He then tied it to one of the carvings and then repeated the process with the other wrist. When he was done, Marco's arms were splayed out across the bed like a martyr.

Ardovan stepped back and turned towards the burning embers of the fireplace. There may be enough heat, he thought to himself, but it's always best to be sure. He walked over, grabbing a handful of kindling from the stockpile to the side and carefully placed it onto the embers. After a few gentle puffs, the flames licked back into life.

The room lit up with a gentle light, but Ardovan ignored it, instead pulled out a small pouch from his belt, and quickly tugged the strings free. Inside was filled with a fine black powder. He withdrew a pinch and slipped the pouch back where it came from. Then standing with his back to the fireplace, facing the bed, he abruptly tossed the powder onto the flames.

There was a mighty whooshing noise and the entire room exploded with a blinding white light, then quickly dimmed. Marco screamed out and tried to desperately cover his eyes, but his tied wrists restricted him. Ardovan stepped forward so that his shadow fell across the squirming form and Marco, after a few moments, suddenly stopped moving, instead he stared at the black outline, a whimper escaped his lips.

"Who, who are?"

"You know who I am Marco Spirensi! I am vengeance! I am death!"

Marco lay there frozen with fear, his mouth worked silently but no sound could be uttered. He closed it and tried to swallow, but there was little moisture.

"Ardovan?" he managed to croak.

Ardovan leapt forward and landed gracefully onto the footrest, his body crouched ready to strike. Marco suddenly found his voice and with an inhuman sound, screamed for his guards. Ardovan smiled coldly and stepped lightly onto the bed "You have no guards, murderer, you have no one." His movements across the bed were deliberate and unhurried until Ardovan straddled the prone man. "But you do have me … and your guilt!"

"Guards! Guards!" screamed Marco, desperation refusing to accept his plight. He violently tried to tear his arms free, but only succeeded in tightening the knots. The skin on his wrists tore and blood started to seep onto the sheets.

Ardovan pulled forth an old rusted dagger from his boot and held it in front of Marco's pallid face. "Do you recognise this, coward?"

Marco stopped screaming and darted looks between the door and the knife. Realisation slowly dawned on him as the knife came into focus and he looked deeply into Ardovan's eyes "Who are you? You—you're not Captain Ardovan!"

Ardovan bit down his anger and in a cold voice uttered, "I was once the son of the most honoured man in this country; a man revered by the public; a man who had stood and defended the King; a man who was murdered in cold blood by a coward who used this very knife to tear his out his throat!" Spittle sprayed out as the last sentence almost came out as a scream.

Ardovan paused and swiftly swallowed back his tears. "My name is … no, was Culowyn Govan. I am the son of Lord Govan! For your treachery to the King and to his loyal servant, I hereby sentence you to death!" Ardovan flipped the knife, so that the blade faced down. Then taking it in both hands, he whispered, "May Hulda forgive you, for I cannot!"

"No!" shrieked Marco.

Just as he was about to drive the dagger down, Ardovan suddenly registered another voice screaming out behind him and a sudden sharp pain lanced into the rear of his shoulder. Falling forward, Ardovan subtlety twisted and grabbed his assailant's arm, pulling the shadowy figure on top of him, whilst at the same time landing heavily on top of Marco.

The figure screeched and dropped a small knife. Acting purely on instinct, Ardovan briskly plunged the rusty dagger into its stomach and then using the momentum, threw the body to the side of the bed, ripping out the blade as it went flying.

The body grunted as it hit the floor hard and a gout of blood shot into the air.

"No, Arcis!" screamed Marco.

Ardovan shot a horrified look over at the bleeding from. It was Arcis. Marco's ten-year-old son. An innocent.

Leaping off of the bed, Ardovan quickly ran to the side of Arcis and carefully turned him over. Blood pooled everywhere. As he examined the savage wound, he realised Acris wasn't going to survive it. The blemished blade had literally torn its way through the stomach and the poor boy's entrails were hanging out in disarray.

Ardovan looked up at Marco and shame hit him hard. "I … I … didn't want to harm him. He's innocent of your crime!" He found he couldn't control his emotions, tears of anger had become tears of guilt.

Marco kept crying out Arcis's name, tears, snot, and spittle running freely across his face. His body twisted, desperate to hold his dying son. Ardovan lifted Arcis as tenderly as he could, but the young boy still moaned aloud as he was carried over to the bed.

Placing him next to his distraught father, Ardovan swiftly cut the bonds from Marco's wrists, who immediately cradled Arcis's head lovingly. Sobs distorted his words. Ardovan stepped back, numb.

Looking down upon father and son, it slowly dawned on Ardovan on what he had become. Sure, he had delivered vengeance. Marco's death would have been brief and painful, but then it would have been over: a release almost. But this, the death of his son, would surely hurt Marco more than any blunted knife ever could. No, this was all wrong, Ardovan's conscious screamed. He had become that which he was avenging. He had become a murderer! A slaughterer of innocents! A monster!

Ardovan turned away and stepped towards the fireplace, his mind in turmoil. He should just give himself up and accept the consequences: he was as guilty as Marco now. But there was another part, deep within his mind that still saw this as the rightful vengeance for the death of his family, his entire family: his father, his mother, Aiden, and Ardovan. All done by the hand of this weeping and pathetic man. His quest was now over. He could start afresh and right this one wrong. Do something positive and find a way to atone for the wrongful death of Arcis.

Ardovan took a deep breath and composed himself. He knew what he had to do and so banished his guilt temporarily before summoning his anger. He felt his core start to burn with the old fury. With gritted teeth, Ardovan pulled free his longsword.

Turning slowly to face Marco, Ardovan purposely strode forward and placed his naked blade against the sniveling man's neck. At first, Marco was too grief-stricken to notice until Ardovan called him by name.

"Marco!" He barked.

Marco looked up but he was not fearful, he was consigned to his sentence and with the death of his son, was almost hopeful for the end to be swift.

"Kill me and be done with it," he uttered.

Ardovan paused and then simply said, "No."

Marco stared at him for a beat and then suddenly screamed with an almost primal bellow, "Kill me!"

"No."

The two men faced each other in silence, both faces a myriad of emotions.

Then after a few moments had passed, Ardovan stated in a cold voice, "I will not kill you tonight for I have reaped my vengeance upon you with the death of your son. But know you this: for every cruelty and crime you commit from this morn on, I shall return and kill a loved one until you are left alone and vulnerable, and then I shall sever your limbs, but I will not kill you. This is the punishment that you once condemned my family to for your own greed, even though we, like your son here, were innocents."

Ardovan slowly withdrew his blade, sliding the razor edge across Marco's cheek, scouring it deeply. Marco didn't flinch.

"That is to remind you that I'll always be watching," said Ardovan and then he turned and slowly made his way towards the balcony.

The morning sun abruptly broke free of the horizon. Marco had to quickly raise his hand to ward off the brilliant light. He parted his fingers to keep watch of Ardovan, but there was no one there.

THE GIFT

The Gift

Gravel crunches as the tires roll to a stop. The car door opens and a figure slowly steps out of the vehicle. Even though it is the middle of the night, there is more than enough light to see due to the cloudless skies and the luminescence of the opulent full moon.

The figure weeps quietly as he gently closes the door. His right hand is clenched tightly and he looks down at it a beat before walking towards the pathway before him. He does not take note of his surroundings; his mind is consumed by the trauma of the moment. Branches that reach out to block his path are ignored, even when some of the thorns tear into his clothing. He has walked down this pathway many times in the past; he could walk it blindfolded. In fact, his first time here was blindfolded, an idea his future wife thought would be quite kinky and insisted upon him participating.

The man stops and groans, quickly dismissing the thought. The pain is too fresh. Roughly wiping his face dry with his sleeve, he takes a deep breath to clear his mind, but he fails and instead sees her face in his mind's eye. She is smiling; her beauty is beyond description. She is reaching out to him, her perfect lips are moving, but he cannot hear her words.

"No!" he screams and breaks into a sprint through the underbrush, hoping to evade any more of the visions of her.

He runs blindly, tears distorting his view. But he is not lost, for there is only one destination here. Minutes later the bushes break apart and release him. He trips and falls heavily down a small escarpment, landing ungainly on the beach.

Lying there, he suddenly releases his tears with an inhuman cry, his body wracked with painful sobs. The aching in his heart is more than he can bear. He feels he needs to retch, but even that is denied him.

He rolls over onto his back and screams out "Why?" as loud as he can. But there is no answer and after a moment or two, he slowly gets to his feet.

The beach is vast and with the silvery light of the full moon, he can see that he is the only person there. The sea is gentle, a flat expanse of black silver. There are no waves nor is there any sound other than the gentle sighs of the wind.

Drinking in the beauty of the scene, the man slowly begins to get a grip on his anguish. He allows the tranquility to seep into his subconscious, just as he had hoped. A small smile slowly breaks through the tears.

"Oh God, Mari, you always love these nights; they're almost as beautiful as you."

Memories resurface, but for the first time that night, they are not painful. He is just an observer of an event four years past.

Shimmers appear near the waterline. As he concentrates, he can see the ghostly images of him and Mari walking arm in arm, splashing through the shallow water as the small waves break upon the shore. Laughter rings out, for they had just been on their first date, and the evening was ending. In a minute, they will kiss for the first time, and he will taste that little piece of heaven.

He had talked nonsense all night and she was teasing him for it, when they both stop walking and look deeply into each other's eyes. Their smiles falter when they both realise what they want to happen, but are unsure of the other's feelings. She reaches up, cupping his face; he leans in tentatively and gently places a tender kiss on her lips. Pulling back, he is pleasantly surprised when she moves in and kisses him back passionately. Her aroma and touch overwhelm his senses. He immediately falls under her spell.

The memory is beautiful. He can't help but smile at it. But something is digging into his hand, disrupting it. Reluctantly, he breaks away from the vision and looks down at his right hand, unclasping it. In his palm is a slim plastic band with a metal grip.

It is a hospital tag. Suddenly he cries out as he is assaulted by his most recent memory as it comes crashing down upon him again.

* * *

His is now standing in a clinically clean corridor. There is chaos all around with porters, doctors, and nurses running about calling out in their own private language. He is lost, and although he is calling out for help, no one hears him. A strong calloused hand settles upon his shoulder and gently turns him around, a wizened face looks down at him, eyes full of sympathy.

The man wants to ask a million questions, but all that comes out of his mouth is, "Why?"

"Sir, you are in shock. You need to sit down."

He allows himself to be guided to a chair, and it is only once he has sat down is he aware that the wizened face belongs to a policeman. A hot cup is passed into his hands, and he remembers that the policeman had gone to get him a cup of tea.

"What happened?"

The policeman looks uncomfortable, but then says, "Your wife was involved in a hit and run. I'm, I'm afraid that when they brought her in, she, um, she wasn't in a very good shape. I'm sorry, sir."

A lump the size of an egg forms in his throat, and he finds himself choking. He still has to ask the question, so he swallows the lump with difficulty. His tears have their own will though. They fall unimpeded.

"Is she, is … is she?" He can't finish the sentence.

"I don't know, sir. What I do know, is they are doing all that they can."

He nods as if he understands, but inside his heart is being ripped apart. The whole world shrinks to the cup of tea he holds. He tries everything he can to hold it together.

He had only seen her a couple of hours ago. She was out visiting a nearby friend. Although they had kissed when she left, he hadn't kissed her properly. He knew this route of thinking was ridiculous; they were both madly in love with each other. They had never said a bad word or felt anger towards each other. In fact, as far as he could remember, they had never argued at all in all the four years they were together. It was clichéd, but he honestly believed she was his soul mate. There would never be another like her. The thought sat there and he found himself repeating it again. There would never be another like her.

He could feel the primal build up of despair begin in his throat. He quickly takes a sip of tea to try and quell it. His eyes burn as he feels the steam mix with his tears. He blinks violently to try and clear them. He has to keep it together.

A voice calls out, as if through a cloud, and then he realises that a doctor is calling out his name. He looks up into the face of a middle-aged man who was about to impart bad news.

"Yeah?" He croaks.

"Mr. Elliott? Can you come with me please. I need to talk to you."

Panic explodes within and he fumbles with the cup spilling its contents onto the floor. The policeman reacts immediately and grabs the cup before it can spill completely. With his other hand, he grips the man's arm for reassurance.

"It's okay, sir, I've got this," says the policeman with veiled relief. "You'd best go on with the doctor."

With leaden legs, the man stands and allows himself be taken down the corridor to a small office on the side. Once inside, he's shown a chair. He sits heavily already knowing the outcome; they were just delaying the inevitable.

"Mr. Elliott," starts the doctor once he seats himself next to the man. He speaks slowly and deliberately, having had to go through this many times in the past. "You must understand that the trauma your wife suffered was very severe. We did everything we could, but I'm afraid it wasn't enough, the damage was too extensive. I'm sorry, but we couldn't save her."

The doctor pauses a while, allowing the news to settle in, but the man is no longer listening.

She is dead.

His Mari is dead.

He couldn't conceive of his life without her, and now she has been taken from him. With the finality of the confirmation, the man suddenly feels completely numb. He's aware he's starting to slowly shake his head even as he tries to stop it.

"If it's any consolation," carries on the doctor, "she wouldn't have suffered as the initial blow to her head would have rendered her uncons—"

"Can I see her?" blurts the man.

The doctor pauses, but then nods and says, "Of course, Mr. Elliott. Though I must warn you there was some external damage you may find distressing."

"MY WIFE HAS JUST DIED! HOW MUCH MORE DISTRESSED CAN I GET?" explodes the man.

It is an uncontrolled outburst. He immediately feels shame. "I'm, I'm sorry doctor. I'm just … I … I just need to say goodbye to … to her."

"I understand, Mr. Elliott." The doctor stands and looking down at the man, says, "I shall prepare her for you to say your farewell." As he opens the door, the doctor turns back to the man and says with genuine sincerity, "I really am sorry for your loss, Mr. Elliott. She was a very beautiful woman. You have my sincere condolences."

The man nods nonchalantly and utters a thank you.

Time slips away and the man sits in a stupor completely oblivious of everything going on around him. His mind races with a thousand memories, each as precious as the next one. He tries to capture each and every one and gift-wrap them before he forgets them. It's the only way he can control his emotions which he can feel bubbling away just beneath the surface. He coverts all of her precious moments, her smile, her eyes, her laugh, her touch, her smell, desperate to remember everything.

It may have been only five minutes or it could have been five hours later when the doctor returns to the office.

"Mr. Elliott?"

But the man doesn't hear him, he slowly rocks in his seat, lost in his memories.

"Mr. Elliott," the doctor repeats more sternly and touches the man's shoulder.

The man jumps and looks up at the doctor expectantly.

"Your wife is ready now."

"I, er, sorry, yes. Thank you."

The man stands and is surprised to feel strength in his legs. He darts quick, little glimpses around the room as he pats down his pockets, hoping to delay the next part. Why did he ask to see Mari? He doesn't want see her blooded face, but another part of him demands it. He needs closure.

The man looks at the doctor and nervously gestures before saying, "After you, doctor."

The doctor smiles sympathetically and leads the man down another corridor. Unconsciously, the man notes that the policeman is still seated at the reception. For some reason, it comforts him. He hasn't been abandoned.

As they enter the private room, the first thing the man notices is they had washed the blood from her face, the rest of her body is covered by a simple white sheet. The man feels gratitude towards the staff as he slowly steps towards his wife. He keeps telling himself that he can do this, but despair sits hungrily near his heart, waiting for the first sign of weakness. His throat constricts as fresh tears spill down his face. As he looks down upon her sweet face, he almost believes she is sleeping until, that is, he touches her. She is cold. Dead cold.

His defenses break down. The man feels an animalistic cry build up from deep inside. He grabs her lifeless hand in his and holds it close to his chest. He leans down and whispers, "Please don't leave me!" just before planting a gentle kiss on her lips. But these too are cold, and he drops his head next to hers as he lets loose a desperate roar of anguish.

The doctor reaches over and gently lifts him from her clutch. He tries to fight the doctor off, but there is no strength left in him. He feels something tug at his right arm. The next thing he is aware of is the presence of the policeman by his side.

"Come sir, there's nothing more that can be done here."

He's lead into an adjacent room where the policeman asks if there is anyone he can contact to take him home. The man shakes his head. He doesn't want to tell anyone just yet, it's still to fresh. Anyway, what would he say, he knew the minute he sat in their car they will look upon him with pity and try and find subjects to occupy his mind, or worse, ask what had happened. He just feels a desperate need to get away and be alone.

Finding a measure of strength inside, the man quietly says, "I'm fine, Officer, I can make my own way home. I, er, I just need to be alone for a while."

"I understand, sir, but I'm afraid I can't leave you alone in this condition. There are staff here who can drive you home." He looks about, but sees no one who can assist him. He leans in to the man and says, "Please bear with me a moment, I'll be back in a little while." And with that the policeman leaves the room.

It dawns on the man this may be his only chance to leave on his own terms, so he waits a beat before getting up, he checks the corridor and sees the usual hustle and bustle, but no sign of either the policeman or the doctor. He steals a quick look back at Mari one last time then hastily exits the room before the lump rises any further and his courage leaves him. The need to get out of the hospital is almost primal; he needs to breath in fresh air. Most importantly, he needs to be alone. His emotions are in a turbulent whorl. He finds it hard to focus on the simplest of things except escape.

As he exits the hospital, dodging the collection of smokers, he spies his car and makes a dash for it. It's not until he sits behind the wheel does he acknowledge he has no destination in mind. He cannot face their home, he's not ready yet, but he needs to be near her, to be somewhere where they shared special moments together, somewhere that was uniquely theirs. And then it occurs to him where he should go.

* * *

The hospital tag sits innocently in his palm and yet this simple piece of flimsy plastic is all the evidence needed to prove Mari's death is real and not some kind of surreal nightmare. The recurrent pain inside riles in anguish, desperate for release. He tries to tame it, but only half-heartedly, he can see no life without her.

He looks out across the ocean and tries to capture the calm that had settled upon him when he first arrived. He finds it too difficult. He closes his eyes and draws in deep breaths, but his concentration breaks when a sigh is heard upon the wind. He opens his eyes and looks down at the water as it gently laps the shoreline. He slowly walks forward, hoping to catch the sigh again. There's a familiarity about it; he knows that sound.

Then he hears it again. It's Mari! She's in the water?

All rational thought evades him as he runs across the beach, ploughing straight into the sea, the water trying to halt his progress. He stops as the cold hits his inner thighs, and he tries to capture Mari's sigh again over his own heavy breathing.

He cries out desperately, "Where are you?"

"Come," the wind whispers back.

His heart jumps. Over there, just a little farther out! He starts forcing his way through the gentle waves ignoring the fact that the sea deepens drastically the farther he advances.

Soon the water strokes his neck, but the thought of him possibly drowning is rapidly quenched when he realises this may be the only way he can stay with her. She's calling out to him so that they can be together forever.

"I'm coming, my love!" he cries out. Trying to tread water, seawater slips into his mouth and he feels the heaviness of his clothes dragging him down. Inadvertently spitting out the sea water, he takes a final look at the moon as it radiates its blessing upon him, and then he lets the water enfold him.

Silence suddenly envelops, and a calm descends all around. His vision is blurred, but he continues swimming into the depths. He knows that the farther he goes he will find her. The evening light colours the sea with an ethereal look. He catches shapes flittering about his peripheral vision. Could one of these beings be her? No, she is straight ahead, that's where her voice came from.

Soon his body starts craving air, but he denies it. Just a little farther, he keeps telling himself, but his arms are not moving so well. They're feeling heavy and his legs struggle to kick out.

Panic begins to take over. His body starts fighting his wishes. It wants air! No! he screams inwardly. She's near! Already he feels his arms fighting to break through to the surface, but it is too far away. He suddenly feels his last gasp of air force its way out of his lungs and no matter how hard he denies it he cannot stop its release. Balls like distorted glass erupt from his throat and rapidly float to the surface leaving him to sink farther into the darkness. His eyes gently close as warmth encloses his body and he finally feels at peace.

I'm sorry, my love.

* * *

The sand feels soft under his naked feet, but his mind refuses to accept this. He knows he was wearing his shoes when he ran into the sea. Still, as he wiggles his toes he feels the tiny grains dance across his skin: dry sand. But that's not possible. He should be at the bottom of the sea, drowned. He remembers the water entering his mouth, its salty flavour suffocating his tongue.

A warm, smooth hand gently takes hold of his. As he tries to look at who is with him, he realises his eyes are closed. Hesitantly, he opens them. He is back on the beach, but the light is strange. Everything is lit with golden-green hue. He looks at the skies and sees the moon still beaming its radiance upon the earth, but it's no longer a brilliant white. Instead, it's an iridescent colour with wispy clouds floating about.

A familiar chuckle beside him causes him to turn and look at who had a hold of his hand. It's an angel, his angel, Mari, alive and giggling.

"Mari?" He reaches up with his other hand and gently cups her face as if afraid to break the vision, but she's real.

"Oh God, Mari!" He pulls her fiercely towards him and loses himself in her embrace. He inhales the aroma of her hair and tastes her skin as he kisses her hard on the nape of her neck. Then he feels her lips push up against his, her tongue eagerly exploring his mouth. It's all so real, so beautiful he can't help but cry. Then he tastes her tears mixing with his.

He wants to hold on to her forever and never let go, but she reluctantly pulls away. She looks deeply into his eyes, her fingers stroking his face and she can't help but smile at him. His mouth opens. He finds it hard to speak. Finally he manages to croak "Please, please don't—"

She interrupts, her smile falters, "Why?"

He's confused by her question. "Why? Why what? What do you mean, why?"

"Why are you trying to kill yourself?"

"I'm not." But then he remembers his feelings of relief as the air escaped his lungs. He looks away ashamed, unable to look at her. "I mean, I wasn't trying to … I didn't want to die, not really, but, but I couldn't bear the thought of living without you and when I heard your voice coming from the sea, I couldn't, I couldn't resist it. You're everything to me."

He looks back at her. "If you wanted me to live, why then, why did you call out to me? Why, if you didn't want me to be here with you dead?" He suddenly realises his grip has tightened on her arm and he hastily relaxes his hands.

Her look is forgiving. She kisses him lightly on the lips. "I didn't call out to you. That was you. Your pain is so acute that you're reaching out for any hope, including taking your own life."

His confusion is written across his face. "But I heard you."

"What you heard was your imagination. Your grief made yourself believe the wind was my voice. God, I would never want you to kill yourself. I love you!"

"So. I'm, er, I'm dead?" He looks out across the ethereal beach uneasily. "And this is … heaven?"

She laughs that perfect laugh of hers with a hint of sadness then shakes her head. "No, darling, you're not dead, at least not yet. But you must go back and soon."

Desperation clutches his heart. "No! We're together. I will not lose you again!"

"We have no choice. If you die in this manner, we will never be together again."

"What?"

"You cannot take your own life, it is too precious a gift. You will be punished if …" Her voice wavers and she swallows back her tears. "If you go back now, we will be together again soon, trust me. Your journey must continue on without me, for a little while at least."

He shakes his head in disbelief. "You make it all sound like there is some kind of plan to all this."

She smiles. "Nothing happens without reason. That's all I can tell you." She pulls him into her arms and holds him tightly. He can feel her heart hammering against his. "As much as I want to stay here in your arms, you must go back."

"How can I continue on without you in my life?"

"Because I'll always be there with you."

"And if this is just a dream? What's to stop me trying to kill myself again?"

She relaxes her grip and looks up at him. "I'll give you a sign. Now go, please, we're leaving it too long as it is."

He looks hard into her eyes and sees her desperation and the incredible control she's fighting to contain. She believes in what she's saying and he realises then he doesn't really have much of a choice. He finally nods. "How? How do I get back?"

She tries to force a smile but is betrayed by her feelings. "You go back the same way you came. Here, you must go back to the sea."

He swallows hard and nods his understanding. He drinks in her beauty then leans down to kiss her one last time.

"I love you so much," he whispers.

"I love you too, Malcolm."

He tries to smile, but finds it too hard. She cries quietly, but her sobs start to build with intensity, and he realises that if he stays any longer, he will never have the strength to leave her.

"I will see you again!" he promises as he forces his fingers to open.

She can't answer him. All she can manage is a small wave.

He doesn't turn away from her the entire time he walks back into the sea. He even tries to keep his eyes open as his head slips under the gentle waves. It is only when he can no longer see her that he lets loose a howl of pain. Air rushes out of his mouth and he inhales water as he breathes back to cry out again.

* * *

He chokes and tries to fight his way back to the surface.

It shouldn't be that far, he's only just submerged his head, but he can't feel it. Frantically, he starts to swim upwards, but his clothes drag him down. Kicking off his shoes, he also manages to pull off his jacket, letting them sink to the murky depths. Suddenly he finds that the struggle lessens and that he's beginning to make progress.

Moments later his head breaks free. He sucks in as much air as his lungs can take. It's too painful, and he violently coughs up phlegm and spit, but seawater crashes back on top of him. He starts choking as his body starts slipping under again. He may have made it to the surface, but he knows he doesn't have the strength to swim back to shore.

Water slams into his mouth a second time. He finds himself panicking as his air supply is cut off. His arms flail, and he feels the depths calling back to him. Suddenly an arm wraps around him and supports him enough to allow him to breath in the precious air. He tries to look at his saviour, but the angle is wrong. All he can do is try to assist whoever it is and make it back to the shore in time.

Painful minutes later, he is finally able to feel the ground beneath his feet. Eagerly, he fights the pull of the waves and forces his way through the water until he is able to fall helplessly to his knees.

Then, on all fours he drags his exhausted body to the dry sand before collapsing and allowing his lungs to fill up with as much fresh air as they demand.

He lies there for long minutes, relishing each breath, eyes closed, when he realises he hasn't thanked his saviour. Slowly he sits up and looks around him. There is no one in sight.

He looks out across the beach, but the moonlight just emphasizes his loneliness. The only sign of anyone being there are his footprints in the sand racing into the sea and the grooves of his body dragging itself out again.

It was nothing but a dream and he feels his despair start to build up again. Will it always be there? He couldn't see any way to stop it. Each and every thought of Mari just brought a fresh wave of hopelessness.

He starts to get up when he notices some extra markings next to the grooves he had made as he exited the sea. He leans closer and recognises the markings as footprints, but they're not his. They're too small, like those of a child or ... a woman.

Hastily he stands up and looks around, hope welling up deep inside. The footprints follow him up to where he collapsed, but then they disappear. They don't go back to the sea, nor do they head back to the footpath. They stop with him.

A voice echoes across his memories.

"I'll give you a sign."

A smile grows on his face. He is not alone, and he never will be. He has found his soul mate, and she'll always be with him.

He turns back to the sea and utters, "I'll see you soon, my love."

A sea breeze kisses his cheek, and he smells her on him.

REDEMPTION

Redemption

The sparkle of the streetlights against the soaked pavement gave the appearance of walking on stars, mused Helen, though her brisk walk destroyed the celestial bodies as her boots splashed through the puddles. For the umpteenth time, she checked her watch, which only confirmed what she already knew: she was late.

Her destination was just across the road, an old dilapidated building that had been bought up by a charity and converted into a shelter for the homeless. Because of the bad weather, Helen could see it was going to be a busy night; already a number of bodies were shambling around the welcoming light of the main window.

The rain started up again. Helen quickly checked the road before she hurriedly ran across the pitted tarmac to take shelter under an adjacent shop awning. The rain was falling harder. She could feel it start to trickle down her back, causing minor shivers to run down her spine.

Pulling up the collar of her old jacket and pulling free her long dark hair, she prepared to cross the final leg of her journey, when one of the figures standing in the doorway of the shelter spied her and called out. It was Bud, an old local. Waving back, Helen shrugged into her jacket further and sprinted across the opening to where Bud stood, holding open the door. She quickly ran past him into the building.

"Thanks, Bud. Looks like the heavens have only just started to open up. It's going to be a real wet one tonight."

"Damn right, Ms. Shepherd."

"Bud, I've told you a dozen times, you can call me Helen. I ain't anyone special." But she already knew he wouldn't call her by anything other than her formal name. He was old school, if ever there was a classification for the homeless. Her best estimate was that Bud was hitting sixty years of age, though with the toll of living off the streets, he could be a lot younger.

"Sure thing, Ms. Shepherd," Bud said as he closed the door. He then headed to a chair near the window, so that he could look out for other escapees from the rain.

Helen smiled at Bud's simplistic job. It wasn't much but it made him feel like he was worth something, and that meant a lot in this world she had found herself in.

Taking off her jacket she made her way over to the kitchen where a number of workers were busily running around preparing the evening meal.

"Hey, Matt, sorry I'm late."

A clean-shaven man turned to Helen's apology and smiled.

"Hi, Helen, no worries. Just glad you could make it." He was the manager of the shelter and although he was young, no older than early thirties, he took the responsibility of the shelter very seriously. "We're running a bit short tonight, so would you mind helping out Sally with the potatoes?"

Helen nodded, then hanging up her jacket and grabbing an apron she made her way over to a middle-aged woman who was expertly shaving the skins off potatoes.

"Hey, Sally, need any help?"

"Well, you're a welcome sight for sore eyes, I must say," laughed Sally. "Thought I'd end up shaving the skin off my fingers before long."

Helen grabbed a knife then leaned in and started peeling. This was her work every night and had been for the past couple of months, volunteering at the shelter. She'd been helping out at a number of shelters for nearly three years now. Little was she to know that something was going to happen very soon that would change all this.

* * *

As Helen had suspected earlier, the thunderous weather had brought all of the stragglers and homeless to the refuge. It wasn't long before the queue stretched and folded in on itself like a coiled snake, taking up most of the open space in the foyer.

For the next hour, Helen and four of her colleagues tirelessly handed out the hot soup they had prepared earlier, along with a steaming cup of tea. With each portion, Helen would laugh and joke with the patrons. At the same time, she would steal a look at their faces, each time silently praying she would find what she was looking for and each time finding only disappointment. As the line thinned down, she noticed one person had stayed away from the queue and was seated, huddled in a darkened corner.

"Matt?"

He was standing to her right handing out the remaining chunks of bread to help soak up the soup, "Yeah?"

"Are you okay to cover me? I want to make sure the guy over there is okay."

"No worries. Here, take some bread to him and grab a bowl on your way over."

Helen gratefully took the bread, ladled some soup into a bowl and made her way over to the figure. It had its back to her and seemed to be cowering in the darkness. Tentatively, she walked up and gently coughed. The figure's back stiffened and slowly turned. It wore a baseball cap under a hoodie, so she couldn't make out what sex it was as most of the face was shadowed.

"Um, I thought you might like some soup?" she asked, holding out the steaming bowl in one hand and the bread in the other. The head looked at the bowl for a beat and then looked up at Helen. The light shone on to the face of a young man.

Helen gently gasped. His face, so young and beautiful, held so much pain. His eyes were sky blue, and his skin was tanned as if sun kissed. His hair, which had escaped part of his hood, was long and golden, and he had the barest beginnings of a beard.

Helen found herself seated, even though she had no recollection of sitting.

The young man reached out and took the bowl in both hands.

"Thank you," he replied with a soft voice.

He then proceeded to drink from the bowl, flinching slightly as the hot liquid touched his lips.

"I, er, I have a spoon here if you'd prefer," mumbled Helen, she couldn't take her eyes from his face.

He shook his head.

"Thanks, but I'm okay," he said softly and continued to drink the rest of the soup. He then took the bread from Helen and used it to clean the remains from the bowl. Although he hadn't queued, it was quite clear he was starving.

"What's your name?" Helen asked, once he had finished eating.

He paused and looked deep into her eyes. She got the impression he was looking for something inside of her. Honesty? She knew from experience that many of the street people rarely trusted others. A homeless shelter was no exception.

He obviously came to a conclusion, because his body retracted into itself as if in fear, or was it shame? His eyes darkened and he reluctantly pulled his gaze away and looked back out of the window into the darkness.

Helen sighed and felt saddened in his reaction towards her. She leaned forward to take the empty bowl from his hands.

"Rowley," he whispered.

She stopped, he was still looking out the window, but from her position, she could see his profile. A glint of light caught his cheek. She realised it was a tear.

"I'm, I'm Helen." She wanted to say more, but couldn't find the words. Instead she said, "I'll be here if you need me," and quietly left him to his sorrow.

Slowly she walked back to the kitchen, her thoughts a jumble. She didn't know why Rowley had affected her so, it's not like she hadn't seen her fair share of sad and lost people in this volunteer service, but there was something about him that transfixed her. Something almost personal.

When she returned to the counter, she noticed the queue had died down to a few latecomers. Matt was alone by the stove having a quiet mug of coffee and reading the late edition of The Herald.

She walked up to him with her back to the crowd. "Matt?" she enquired quietly.

"Yeah?" He looked up with a smile, then saw the concern in her expression. He immediately put down his coffee.

"Are you okay?" That was the thing about Matt, he was always willing to listen, no matter what he was doing. He was the soul of the shelter; he would willingly give his time to each and every one of his customers and in doing so would greet each person by name. He had been doing this work for most of his adult life and knew the people in this area like they were his own family. In a way, they were.

"That guy over there," Helen pointed over her shoulder to Rowley. "He said he was called Rowley, do you know anything about him?"

He subtly shifted himself to look behind Helen. "Hmm, not much, he started coming here about the same time you started. I'm surprised you haven't noticed him before. Oh wait, no you wouldn't have. You only work the night shift don't you? Well, he usually comes in during the day. Come to think of it, I think this is the first time I've ever seen him in here this late. I always wondered where he went during the night. The guy's really shy. He doesn't talk much." Matt looked back at Helen. "He must have taken a real shine to you if he told you his name, it took me three weeks to get it out of him. All I know is that he's haunted by something bad. Some terrible incident must have happened to him, poor kid."

Helen looked back at Rowley, a deep sadness seeping its way into her heart.

"Yeah, poor kid," she whispered.

* * *

She didn't see Rowley for the next four days, even though she looked out for him. According to Matt, he hadn't come in during the daytime either. She started to be concerned for his safety, what if something had happened to him? She found herself asking the regulars if they had seen him. All had said that they hadn't, though this wasn't unusual, they each lived their own lives, some preferring their solitude. It was obvious that Rowley was one of these individuals. It didn't quell her anxiety for him any less.

Then, on the fifth evening, she saw his hunched figure enter and briefly talk to Bud, before walking over to the shadowed corner to sit alone and look out the window. She immediately stopped what she was doing, grabbed some bread and went over to him, although she pulled herself up short just behind him and took a deep breath.

"Hi, Rowley, haven't seen you in a while."

She received no response; he just kept looking out of the window. Feeling a bit awkward, Helen quickly sat down beside him and hesitantly handed out the bread. "Are you hungry?"

He slowly looked from the window to the bread and then up at Helen's face, his beautiful blue eyes once more peered intensely into her, as if looking directly into her soul, she almost felt naked in his presence. It was the sadness that radiated from his gaze that cut her most deeply.

Her hand trembled and started to lower.

Rowley reached out and took the bread.

"Thank you," he whispered.

He gingerly bit into it and turned back to looking out the window.

The minute he turned away, Helen felt herself being released. She wasn't afraid of him. On the contrary she felt a kinship with him, but his torment was almost too much. Helen sat in silence watching Rowley as he slowly picked the bread apart and then taking tiny bites. It was almost hypnotic the way he moved. She found herself asking herself again, why was she so fascinated with him. What was it that was so captivating? And more importantly, what tragic event had happened that haunted Rowley so much?

"You are married, Mrs. Shepherd."

She was so distracted with her own thoughts it took a moment before his words settled in.

"What?"

Rowley shifted round to face her. "'I said that you are married."

She realised it wasn't a question. She sat there stunned, looking at him.

"How do you know that? No one here knows."

"You have the look of someone who knows love."

He must have realised he had startled her as he suddenly smiled. It was a beautiful smile that lit up his face; his eyes lost their haunted look and became warm and inviting.

He pointed to her finger. "I saw a ring imprint on your wedding finger when you handed me the bread. I take it you remove it each night when you work here?" His smile wavered a bit. Helen realised she hadn't changed her expression. Torment slowly descended upon his face like a shadow and his warm smile vanished.

"I'm sorry," he whispered and started to move back to the window. Helen reached out and touched his arm.

"No, no, I'm the one who's sorry. You're just stating what you saw and naturally drew a conclusion." She brushed some loose strands of hair from her face and folded her hand under her other one in her lap, unconsciously covering up the offending digit.

She took a deep breath. Out the corner of her eye, she noticed one of the streetlights had a fault and was blinking in the darkness. She watched it flicker as she gathered her thoughts.

"You're right. I, I am married, but I haven't seen my husband in a long time."

A moment passed then Rowley's soft voice asked, "What happened?"

Helen nervously chuckled. "Aren't I supposed to be asking you that question?"

"Sometimes people forget it's not just the homeless who get lost."

She turned back to Rowley to find his warm gaze upon her.

"Why would a complete stranger care about me?" she said.

Rowley reached out to tentatively touch Helen's hand, but stopped midway. Instead, he returned it to the folds of his dirt-encrusted jacket.

"I hear that each night you come out here selflessly, to help those who are lost and alone—all of them complete strangers. You offer them a home. You listen to their cares and worries, yet you have no one to listen to yours."

Helen sat there looking intently at him; he was sincere. She could feel he genuinely wanted to help, the sadness in him was part of it. Memories came flooding back with a rush, along with all the emotions she had buried deep within her. Helen took another deep breath to try and control the flood, but she knew she wouldn't be able to hold it back for long. She hadn't talked about this in such a long time and yet here she was, about to open her heart to a young man whom she has only just met.

"My husband, he, um, he left about three years ago after we, er, we …" Talking was becoming difficult with the lump that was growing in her throat. She closed her eyes; welled tears broke free. She could still clearly see the pain in her husband's eyes as he walked out the front door. "Something terrible happened. It broke our relationship. I, um, I was willing to get help, to see someone, but it was too much for him. Then one day, he went out, he, um, he never came back." Tears were flowing freely now.

"Is that why you are out here? Hoping to find your husband?" There was a catch in Rowley's voice. Helen opened her eyes. A single tear ran its course down his bearded cheek. Why should he be feeling her pain? He knew nothing about her. What did he know that she didn't?

"Yes. Why? Do you know where he is?"

He didn't answer, instead he lowered his head as if in shame.

Another moment of silence pasted. "The tragedy that tore you apart. What was it?" Rowley asked.

"It's very personal. And although it's been … a long time … and I appreciate your wish to help, it's still very fresh."

Rowley nodded slowly, understanding. "I'm sorry if I've distressed you."

Helen could only nod through her tears. And so they sat in silence, both looking out at the streetlights lost in their own thoughts.

After a while, Rowley got up. He looked down at the anguished face of Helen as she stared off into the distance. He went to reach out to touch her hair, but stopped himself. Instead, he closed his hand and put it back in his pocket before walking out of the shelter.

Helen sat at the window for the rest of the night lost in her memories. Matt and the others could see she needed time to herself, so they left her there undisturbed.

* * *

The next couple of days went by uneventfully, though Matt could see Helen had become withdrawn. Although she was still courteous and polite to the patrons, her sparkle had dimmed, and the laughter was now forced.

Rowley had also come in each night, but Helen had stayed away from him, she didn't even acknowledge him. One night, Matt had gone up to Rowley to see what had happened, but all he could get out of him was that it was some personal matter.

Then one night Matt spied Helen glancing over at Rowley, it was the first time she'd looked at him since the night the two of them had talked. She seemed to be torn over whether to walk over to him or not. Wandering over, he stepped up beside her.

"How you're holding up?" he asked.

"Wh? Oh, hi, Matt. I'm fine," she said sheepishly. Although she looked up at him and smiled, it was forced, and she kept glancing over to the back of Rowley. The tea towel in her hands was slowly being twisted into a tightrope.

"Hey, It's not like me to interfere, but it seems to me you and Rowley need to sort a few things out. Did he, er, say anything … I don't know, offensive to you?"

Helen kept her eyes on Rowley, but shook her head. "No, no, not at all. He just made me remember … something important."

When she briefly looked up, Matt saw her eyes were pink, as if on the verge of crying. He reached out, took the tortured tea towel from her hands, and replaced it with a piece of kitchen paper he'd just grabbed from the counter. He then gently pushed her towards Rowley. "Then I suggest you go talk to him."

She allowed herself to be pushed a little of the way, then stopped and took a deep breath. She glanced back at Matt with half a smile.

"Yeah, I think I will."

* * *

A small photo that had obviously been kept lovingly within a wallet or purse was put in front of Rowley. It was a picture of a laughing young boy wearing a Yankee's baseball cap. The edges were frayed and torn slightly as though it had been handled a lot.

"His name was Justin."

Rowley didn't react when he heard Helen's quiet voice behind him. He just reached out and tenderly picked up the picture. He kept staring at the boy's carefree face as Helen sat down next to him.

"He'd be fourteen now."

Rowley returned the photo to Helen. "He looked very happy," he said.

"Yes, yes he was." She peered at it as fresh tears flowed down her cheeks.

"My husband, Geoff, was, well, he was driving home after, um, after picking up Justin, from school. The two of them were playing around, as they usually did and, er, Geoff, must've lost …" Helen shrugged one shoulder and wiped her cheek with the tissue and then the back of her hand. "Oh God, it's been so long since I talked about this." She quickly straightened her back and gazed upwards, trying to compose herself.

Rowley leaned over and without any hesitation, placed a sympathetic hand on her shoulder. She touched his hand with hers and smiled her thanks.

"There was another car," she continued, "that had come out from nowhere. Geoff didn't see, he … he knew he should have been paying more attention. The cars collided and, well, Geoff survived with a minor concussion, a broken arm and some fractured ribs. The other driver, he died not long after. They said that there was massive internal damage. The car was old and didn't have an airbag."

Rowley looked away, pained, and withdrew his hand. Helen took no notice, she was reliving the time.

"They found my baby on the pavement by the side of the road. He had been thrown—" a sob escaped. Helen dropped the photo on her lap and covered her face with her hands. "Oh God," she wept, and after a second grabbed Rowley and buried her face into his shoulder.

At first Rowley tensed, but then visibly relaxed and gently held her close. A few moments later, Helen seemed to have composed herself a bit and pulled away from Rowley.

Wiping her face with her hands, the tissue sodden, Helen averted her eyes from Rowley as she said, "Oh God, I'm so sorry. I didn't mean to let it get to me. I haven't spoken to anyone about this since Geoff …"

"It's okay."

"Thank you, you're very kind." Helen smiled. She fidgeted for a while and put the wet tissue on the table beside her. All the while, Rowley sat there patiently waiting.

Helen glanced at him briefly. "Geoff kept blaming himself," Helen continued. "We'd get into arguments, stupid ones really, over trivial things. Then one day, he said goodbye and was gone. I thought he would return, you know, get away for a bit, sort his head out. But a week quickly turned into a month, which then became two. I soon realised he wasn't going to come back. So, I decided to come out and look for him. I tried all the usual haunts, but I couldn't find anything. Then one evening I watched a program on TV about charities for the homeless people, it explained that a lot of homeless had come from all walks of life, through situations not of their choosing.

"It then dawned on me that Geoff may have become one of them. So I signed up to as many local shelter as I could, to volunteer myself, and, well, I've been searching ever since. Obviously, I've been moving around a bit, doing some work here and there. I needed to open the net as wide as possible," she trailed off and looked around her.

She noticed Matt leaning back at the bar, a wash towel over his shoulder, his arms crossed, watching the two of them carefully. She smiled to him to let him know that she was okay, and he waved back.

"I'd like to help," Rowley said, pulling Helen's attention back to him.

She looked at him "Why?"

"I … need to." He looked uncomfortable as if he was struggling with something. "I know these streets and I know these people."

Helen regarded him for a moment. His pain was palpable. Raw and fresh, just like hers, but at the same time, she could see something else. Was it hope, possibly?

Maybe he really did need to do this just as much as she did.

She nodded perceptively. "Why not."

Rowley smiled and suddenly stood up.

"Thank you," he said and then left hurriedly as if the devil was behind him.

* * *

True to his word, for the rest of the month Rowley asked everyone he could, tirelessly patrolling the streets and the hidden crevices of the city. On a couple of the nights, he even asked Helen to accompany him so she could help identify Geoff. Unfortunately, the city was such a large place. None of the people Rowley had found were her missing husband.

Helen started to despair. In the three years she'd been looking, she realised she hadn't covered even half the ground Rowley did in the single month she knew him. It was as if there was another world out there, another city lying just beneath the one she had always known. But the dangers there were ever more present and threatening than in her world. In her world, she could at least call on the police or any of the other services to come to her aid, but not out there, you had to learn quickly and adapt.

Some nights she found herself wondering if Geoff was still alive, but she quickly quelled those fears. She couldn't allow herself to accept this; she firmly believed that if anything had happened to him, she was sure she would have felt something. She had to believe in that.

What had surprised her was that a lot of the people she had met in the past three years were all willing to help Rowley find Geoff. All of them sympathized with her plight, they all had stories that echoed hers in some way.

* * *

Then one evening, Rowley burst into the shelter, nearly knocking over poor Bud who'd been attempting to open the door for him, and made a beeline straight for the counter where Helen was serving soup.

"I think I found someone who's seen Geoff!" he reported.

The man standing with his back to Rowley jumped out of his skin and almost dropped his bowl.

He turned to face Rowley and growled, "Oi! get t' the back of the line, ya thievin' shit!"

Rowley ignored him. "There's a girl I know, who said that she saw someone of Geoff's description with the same name."

Helen had been caught unawares. She felt herself becoming flustered as her heart rate suddenly soared.

"What? Where?" Her hands shook, and she ended up spilling the ladle of soup back into the saucepan.

"Down Mercer Street. I need you to come!" Rowley held out his hand to her. She looked at it and then at Matt who was standing to her right.

"Hell, if he's found a clue to finding your missing husband, then I'd take it," Matt said. "Anyway, I'm sure we can survive without you for a few hours."

She smiled at him and tried to take off her apron, but she was all fingers and thumbs.

"Here," said Matt, "let me do that." He quickly managed to untie the knot, allowing Helen to take it off.

She handed it to Matt. "Thank you."

He just smiled back and watched as she left the shelter with Rowley.

Once outside, Rowley lead Helen down the road at a brisk pace. "Where is Mercer Street?" she asked

"Just over two miles north of here, near The Imperial."

It took about forty minutes for them to cover the distance. Helen wasn't nearly as fit as Rowley, and she found it hard trying to keep pace with him. After the first ten minutes of marching, Rowley had to slow down to allow Helen time to catch her breath.

* * *

Mercer Street wasn't so much a street as an alley, but one of those alleys that civilization seemed to have forgotten. It was strewn with bits of cardboard, materials, and recycled waste, each piece had been used to create some form of shelter, but the recent rains had turned most of it to mush.

Even though Helen had been out a couple of times with Rowley to question people in the past, she still found it hard seeing people living in this state of squalor. She couldn't help but imagine Geoff living in his own filth. Her heart lurched, he deserved better. They all did.

Rowley soon led Helen to a piece of corrugated steel that was leaning to one side of the street. An old blanket had been draped over the front, creating a makeshift door.

"Gwen," Rowley called out.

There was no answer, so he called out again.

The blanket was pulled aside by a pale skinny hand and a young girl, no more than fourteen years of age, peeked her head out.

"What? Oh, hey, Rowley."

Her long blonde hair, which must have once had a beautiful sheen, was now lank and greasy. Her eyes were sunken with a dead look to them; they were too old for a young teenager. There were a number of bruises on her arms and a particularly bad one round her neck that lead Helen to the conclusion she had been abused, and recently by the looks of it. Her clothes were torn revealing pale bruised skin beneath.

Rowley was just as surprised as Helen when he saw her. "Damn, Gwen! What the hell happened?"

"Nothing much, just Troy and Spitz."

"What did they want?"

"Same as you. That guy you were asking about earlier, Geoff? Looks like he pissed 'em off summut fierce." She looked Helen over with disdain. "This her?"

"Yeah. Look, do you know why they were after for him?"

"Dunno. Something to do with their territories. You know how anal Troy gets."

Rowley sighed. "Yeah, I do. So, where did they go?"

"Down there," Gwen pointed further down the street. "I told 'em I saw their guy down near Larry's."

"And where did you really see this Geoff?"

"As I told 'em. Down near Larry's."

"Ah shit, Gwen!" Rowley cried out. "What were you thinking? You knew I was looking for him."

"Hey! Troy had me by the fucking throat! What did d'ya expect me to do?" she screamed back. "Who's gonna fucking protect me when he finds out I sent 'em on some merry goose chase? Eh?"

"You know I would've been there for you. Ain't I always?"

Gwen looked down suddenly sheepish. "Yeah, I know. Look you better hurry if you wanna catch 'em. They were looking seriously pissed off, and I don't know what they're gonna do when they catch 'im."

"Okay, Gwen, you get back inside and get warm. I'll be back later."

"Yeah, sure," said Gwen as she slipped back inside her makeshift hut.

Rowley grabbed Helen's hand tightly. "Come on, we've got to run!"

Helen felt her panic start to rise as she started to run with him. "Rowley? Are these guys serious?"

"Yeah, if it's Geoff they're after, then we ain't got much time."

Although frightened and tired, Helen's hope at finally finding Geoff lent her the energy needed to keep up with Rowley as he raced them through the streets.

It turned out that Larry's was an old greasy spoon cafe that was now closed and hadn't been open in quite some time. The street was empty except for a few parked cars, but other than that, there was not a soul in sight.

"Damn it!" spat Rowley. "They've got to be somewhere 'round here."

Helen spied a couple of side alleys leading off from the street. "Hey, what about those?" she asked, pointing them out.

Rowley stopped walking round in a circular motion and looked over at where Helen was indicating. "Okay, sure, but stay close."

The two of them jogged over to the first alley and Rowley, pushing Helen behind him, entered the darkened entrance. The alley was just big enough for a car to drive down and had no lights. Placed at various points sat large dumpsters that restricted the view. Rowley led Helen down about fifty feet when a cry of pain suddenly rang out behind them.

Simultaneously, they both realised it hadn't come from this alley. Without hesitation and in tandem, they ran back to the main street and entered the second alley. This one wasn't much different to the first, except there were now a couple of silhouettes moving in the distance.

"I'll teach you, you little fucker!" shouted one of the figures as it started to violently kick what appeared to be a heap on the tarmac. "No one fucks with me, ya' hear?"

Rowley instantly sprang into action and sprinted over to the two standing figures.

"GET AWAY FROM HIM YOU BASTARDS!" screamed Rowley as he threw himself into the standing silhouettes. The three fell into a heap, and Helen lost track of Rowley. It was much too dark, and everything was happening at once. All she could hear were a lot of grunting noises and what sounded like punching.

Then she saw the heap struggle up to its feet and, a moment later, lash out with its foot at one of the protruding heads. "Take that, you fuck!" it croaked.

The voice was strained as if it was unused to being used, but she recognised it instantly. It was a voice she heard every night in her dreams and one that she was dreading she wouldn't ever hear again.

"Geoff?"

The stricken figure used the side of the dumpster to steady itself before it lashed out again. "Fuck you!"

"Geoff!" screamed Helen.

The figure staggered at her cry and turned to face her.

To the side, two figures pulled themselves up from the fight on the floor, it looked like one of them was hurt badly by the way it held its side. She heard one of them call out, "Fuck, he's not alone! Let's get the fuck outta here!"

Grabbing each other, they staggered off into the distance.

"Helen?" the figure gasped.

Upon hearing her name, she knew immediately it was Geoff. At first her legs wouldn't respond, but slowly and surely they started moving. Soon she was running towards him, tears streaming down her face. "Oh God, Geoff!"

He opened his arms and she flew into him. "It's you, it's really you!" she kept crying out as he enfolded her with his embrace.

"Oh God, Helen, I had given up ever seeing you again. I'm so ashamed," but his voice became stifled with his own sobs as he buried his face into her shoulder.

Although she was aware of the dirt that encrusted him and the smell of

unwashed body odor, she didn't care. Her
Geoff was back in her arms … alive. She
wanted to lose herself in him, but a moan of
pain to her left tore through her blissful
thoughts, and Helen suddenly realised that
Rowley was still on the floor.

Reluctantly, she pulled herself away
from Geoff and looked to the ground.

"Rowley?"

Rowley was hunched over in a fetal
position. He tried moving, but stopped
suddenly. His body shuddering, he looked hurt.

"Damn," he muttered.

Helen went to her knees beside Rowley
and gently turned him over onto his back. She
suddenly gasped when she saw that his
stomach was soaked. Gingerly, she touched
the wet material; it was warm and sticky.

"Rowley?" her voice wavered.

"I, I think I've been hurt."

"Oh my God, Rowley. You, you're
bleeding!"

"Yeah, one of them had a knife."
Suddenly Rowley spasmed. "God! It hurts!"
he cried.

Helen quickly took off her jacket,
rolled it up, and pushed it against Rowley's
stomach. She didn't know if it would help,
but they all seem to do it on the TV cop
shows she used to watch.

Geoff crouched down next to her.

"Dear Lord, don't you dare let him die on me," Helen prayed.

"I, I don't know what to say," said Geoff. "You saved my life and brought my wife ba—" he stopped short as the moonlight caught Rowley's face.

"Oh Jesus! No, it can't be!" he stumbled back and sat heavily onto the tarmac.

Helen looked across and saw a look of pure terror on Geoff's face.

"What is it Geoff?"

Geoff pointed shakily at Rowley's pain wracked body. "I know that face! It, it haunts me each night!"

"What do you mean he haunts you? He helped me find you."

"That's not possible, I saw you die!" he cried.

"Geoff, what are you talking about? I'm right here, I never died." Helen's panic at Rowley's wound became fear in seeing her husband's reaction.

"No! Not you—him!"

Confused, she reached out to Geoff. "Geoff, he can't be dead. He's right here, he saved your life, and helped me find you."

"No, he died!"

"Geoff!"

"He's the driver that killed Justin, Helen! I SAW HIM DIE!" screamed Geoff.

"But—"

A blood soaked hand grasped Helen's arm weakly.

"Helen, he's right," Rowley croaked.

Helen slowly turned to face Rowley, her face stunned.

"What?"

"I was that driver … I died."

"But, but how? You're here … alive?"

Through his pain, Rowley smiled. "I was given a chance of redemption to save what I had destroyed. It was me that should have paid more attention, not Geoff."

"But I can touch you."

"Oh God, I'm so sorry, Helen, for all the pain I put you and Geoff through. Please forgive me." Rowley coughed and his body spasmed in pain, black blood seeped out through his lips.

Rowley feebly squeezed her arm. "Don't lose your love for each other. Justin is happy where he is. He loves you both very much," he whispered, his voice became weaker with each breathe. "I have done all I can, Lord."

His breathing stopped.

Helen sat there in a puddle completely stunned, staring at the motionless form of

Rowley. It was happening too quickly, her thoughts were in complete disarray as she desperately tried to sort out what had just been revealed.

Geoff regained some of his composure and leaned forward to touch his wife. "Helen?"

"He was my friend," she said toneless.

He nodded his understanding and took hold of Rowley's blood-stained hand still clasping Helen's forearm.

Suddenly he jerked his hand back, dropping the hand. "What the?"

Rowley's skin had started to glow with a shimmering golden light. At first, it started as gentle sparkles, but quickly grew into strong shards of light that burnt through the skin, illuminating the startled faces of Helen and Geoff. Both of them backed up against the dumpster as Rowley's body was rapidly consumed in the burning light. Helen shaded her eyes with her hand as the light intensified.

A few moments later, the light diminished.

Helen slowly lowered her arm and saw that Rowley's body was no longer there. Even the clothes had disappeared.

"What just happened?" Helen whispered.

"I don't know Helen, but let's get out of here. Let's go home."

The word "home" caught Helen's attention and she held onto Geoff tightly. "Yes, let's go home."

As the two of them entered the main street, Helen stopped and looked back. "Goodbye, Rowley."